MISADVENTURES IN A THREESOME

BY
ELIZABETH HAYLEY

MISADVENTURES IN A THREESOME

BY
ELIZABETH HAYLEY

WATERHOUSE PRESS

This book is an original publication of Waterhouse Press.

Cover Design by Waterhouse Press.
Cover images: Shutterstock

PRINTED IN THE UNITED STATES OF AMERICA

ISBN: 978-1-64263-081-7

For Scott, our editing Swolemate

CHAPTER ONE

"One more rep. You got this!" Maddox encouraged the woman on the workout bench as she pressed two dumbbells into the air above her chest. "Hell yeah! Good work." He grabbed the weights from her hands as she sat up.

"I don't know why I let you abuse me like this," Blake groused as she struggled to reach for her water that was just beyond her grasp. Instead of getting up, she leaned precariously off the bench until she was nearly parallel to the floor.

"Because all you talk about is how you want to look good in your wedding dress," he replied, scooping up her water and handing it to her so she didn't end up sprawled on the floor... again. This girl was seriously something else, though Maddox couldn't deny he got a kick out of the tiny redhead.

"I'm starting to question my priorities," she said.

"Too late now. You're already committed."

"I feel like I *should be* committed for signing up for this. If I wanted to be tortured, I'd go down to that place on Fourth Street that pretends it's just a cocktail lounge. With the amount of leather I've seen walking into that place, it would probably be more economical for them to start skinning their own cows."

Maddox laughed and grimaced simultaneously. He knew

the place she was referring to, and he also knew they hosted leather nights in the back part of the club every so often. Not because he'd been but because his best friend and co-owner of Transform Gym, Wilder, knew everything and everyone in town. They'd talked about going down and checking it out one night, but it really wasn't either of their scenes.

Maddox had always been more inclined to turn his pain inward than inflict it on others, and it was much too serious for fun-loving Wilder. They also both preferred to keep relationships casual, which tended to negate the level of trust-building that was required in BDSM.

"Let's go do some abs, and then you can get out of here," Maddox told her, walking away before she could argue.

Trailing after him, she argued anyway. "Why do we keep having the same conversations? I don't *have* abs. How can I work on something I don't even have?"

"It'll help you get them." He grabbed an ab mat and a medicine ball and led her over to an empty section of the gym.

"I'm not saying I don't have defined ones. I'm saying I don't have that muscle group at all. I was born without them. I'm an anomaly."

"You're an anomaly, all right. Lie down."

"I feel like it's not a compliment when you say it," she muttered as she flopped back on the mat.

Maddox handed her the ball and instructed her through a variety of exercises to strengthen her core. Despite her grumbling, she always did everything he asked of her, which made Maddox enjoy working with her.

As he counted her reps, he saw movement out of the

corner of his eye. He turned his head, and his eyes went wide as he caught a glimpse of Wilder marching through the gym with a sledgehammer slung over his shoulder.

"Wilder! What the fuck are you doing?"

♦♦♦♦

Wilder Vaughn ignored his business partner as he strode purposely toward the portion of their gym that remained empty. He was a man on a mission, and that mission was forcing Maddox's hand. Mad was the best guy Wilder knew, but Jesus Christ he could drive a saint to drink. Or to wield a sledgehammer.

"I'm knocking down walls." The walls in question were attached to a neighboring business the men had purchased over six months ago. After the sale had gone through, they'd begun to gut the place, only for Maddox to dig in his heels when they'd gotten to the point when they'd have to bring in outside help. But no more. Today they'd make some decisions regarding the space if Wilder had to put holes in every wall in the gym.

"I'll be right back," Wilder heard Maddox say to Blake.

"Please don't hurry on my account," Blake said.

Maddox appeared just as Wilder walked through the tarp blocking off the unfinished portion of the gym. He reached out and grabbed the handle of the sledgehammer that had been resting on Wilder's shoulder. "Where did you even get this?" he asked as he tried to wrestle the tool away from Wilder.

The two men locked stares and grips as they battled for control of the sledgehammer, which would ultimately decide who would have control of the entire situation. Control was something Maddox clung to, while Wild was typically content to hand over the reins. Except when it affected his livelihood. Or when Maddox was being a stubborn ass.

Wilder understood Mad's reticence. A lot could go wrong with a remodel and expansion, and the unknown tended to scare the ever-living fuck out of Maddox. There were no guarantees in the fitness business. A gym could be hot one minute and desolate the next. But Wild and Mad had owned a thriving business for almost eight years. Growing it was the next logical step, and if Wild needed to beat Mad over the head with his hammer to see reason, then so be it. "I bought it," Wild gritted out. "If you won't hire someone to expand the gym, I'll do it myself."

Maddox barked out a laugh. "You can't even hang a shelf without it falling down within twenty minutes."

"Right. Which is why I'll be perfect at demo work." Wilder gave a tug on the sledgehammer, gritting his teeth.

"You don't even know which of those walls are load-bearing." Maddox gripped his hands around the mallet, refusing to let go.

Wilder planted his feet and fell backward with all his weight as he pulled. "I'll figure it out," he bit out through the exertion of trying to wrangle the object away from Maddox. *Goddamn, this fucker is strong.*

With a smirk, Maddox let go of the hammer, causing Wilder to crash to the floor.

"You dickhead," Wilder yelled as he scrambled up and reached for the tool he'd dropped. When he had it, he bolted down the hall.

"You're so fucking juvenile," Maddox called after him as he gave chase. He reached Wilder just as he'd pulled the sledgehammer back like a baseball bat, ready to take a swing at the drywall. Maddox threw himself between the wall and hammer just as Wilder began his swing.

Wilder barely had time to react, letting go of the hammer and sending it flying to the right in an effort to avoid hitting Mad. "Are you crazy? I could've killed you." Which was kind of what Wild felt like doing in the wake of Maddox's stupidity.

"You've been slowly doing that for years."

"Funny guy," Wilder muttered as he walked over to the hammer and picked it up. He turned back to Mad. "We need this space, Mad. And I'm tired of waiting for you to let someone in here."

Maddox sighed, and Wilder knew he was wearing his friend down. This topic had been a weekly argument for the last six months. Their gym was functional and had a solid client base, but both men agreed they could attract more people if they increased their offerings. Currently, they had one large multipurpose room that had a variety of classes cycle through it, which could be problematic when a Zumba class followed kickboxing and they had to rush to get the equipment out in time.

They intended to use the extra space to build a yoga studio and a bigger spin room. But while Wilder had been able to convince Maddox to purchase the place, Maddox's anxiety had forced the renovations to halt. Maddox didn't do well with change. Wild knew that.

Mad was a thinker—an overanalyzer, really—and a

chronic worrier. In his quest for perfection, he'd found himself unable to make any progress on the project. Something that was making "act now, worry later" Wilder insane.

Scrubbing a hand over his face, Maddox looked at Wilder. "I'll call the contractor as soon as I'm done with Blake."

Wilder's eyes widened like he was a kid on Christmas morning. "For real?"

"Yes. I swear." Maddox and Wilder had already had someone in who'd come highly recommended. All that needed to be done was officially hire the guy and his crew.

"So I can put some feelers out for some new class instructors?" Wilder was nearly bouncing with excitement. This was the moment he'd been waiting for—the one where he'd turn their little gym into a state-of-the-art fitness facility and they'd move from their two-bedroom apartment into neighboring palatial estates.

"Knock yourself out."

"Hell yeah!" Wilder yelled as he kissed the top of the sledgehammer. "I knew this baby would get your attention."

"Such an asshole," Maddox muttered.

"An asshole who gets to hire some new instructors," Wilder called over his shoulder as he walked away, his gait light and bouncy. Wild could guess how Mad was feeling. He recognized the flexing of Mad's fingers and ramrod straightness of his spine for what it was: a man trying to quell his anxiety.

And while Wild had no interest in sending Mad spiraling into a full-blown panic attack, he did think Mad needed a push every now and then. Sometimes it was the only way to break him out of his rigid mold and get him moving so life didn't pass him by. But Wild also knew when to take his victory and run. "I'll be in the office drafting some ads if you need me."

CHAPTER TWO

The first time Jasmine Pritchett interviewed for a job, she was fourteen years old and had thought getting paid minimum wage at the local pizza shop would result in her financial independence. It hadn't. And now, at twenty-five, she found herself in a similar predicament: hoping *this* job would result in financial independence. Thankfully, according to one of the owners of the gym, the position paid significantly more than her low-paying pizza shop gig.

The man who now sat across a desk from her had introduced himself as Wilder. He was at least a foot taller than her five-four frame and had enough muscle on his body to make him appear even larger than he already was. From behind a pair of reading glasses he'd put on when they'd sat down, he studied her résumé closely. His light hair was shaved close on the sides into a high fade, and the longer top was styled into textured, messy spikes. As he played with his bottom lip, she noticed the nuanced hues of his short beard: blonds to light reds with a few grays even. She wondered how old the man was.

She also wondered if he was thinking she was underqualified for the trainer position. Surely she was. Though she had several fitness certifications, Jasmine's experience in the field was minimal, as was her education. She didn't hold a bachelor's degree or even an associate's in sports science—or in anything, for that matter.

What she did have that she hoped would give her a leg up on her competition was persistence. She'd never been one to retreat just because the opposing army seemed stronger. And she didn't plan on backing down this time either. If these men questioned her abilities, she'd prove herself one way or another. Even if it involved getting the larger of the two into a firefly pose, which—now that she thought about it—she'd actually like to witness.

Jasmine smiled at the other man who had introduced himself earlier as Maddox. There wasn't much else to do, since Wilder was still reading her résumé. She wasn't sure if that was a good sign or a bad one, but she hoped that if they weren't interested, they wouldn't have bothered calling her in the first place. She'd only been here ten minutes, and things already felt unbearably awkward.

Maddox wasn't sure what to do with his eyes. Wilder had been looking at this woman's résumé for at least a full five minutes, which was way too long, especially since Maddox assumed Wild would've looked at her résumé *before* calling Jasmine in for an interview.

Now Maddox was stuck exchanging glances with the dark-haired woman as if the two of them were participating in some sort of reverse staring game. The instant the two made eye contact, it was a race to see who could look away first without appearing as though they were doing so. Maddox cleared his throat and held out his hand to Wild—an act intended to move the interview along. Maddox also wanted something to look at other than Jasmine's dark-green eyes, which already transfixed him.

He took notice of the way her fingers rubbed against her palms as if they had a mind of their own, and he wondered if she was nervous. He hoped it was the silence that had her uneasy and not Maddox's stern demeanor. There was no doubt the army had hardened him, changed Maddox in a way that caused him to stay on guard when he didn't need to, and unfortunately that backfired on him from time to time—especially around people who didn't know him.

"You have a pretty extensive résumé, Ms. Pritchett." Wilder offered her a smile before handing the paper to Maddox, for which he was thankful.

"I do?"

Her reply sounded like a question, and Maddox could only guess that was because her previous work experience ranged from helping the elderly with chores to cutting hair to selling essential oils. Thankfully she did have a few certifications that qualified her to coach classes at Transform, or Maddox would've wondered why the hell Wild had called her in. Though the picture of her at the top of the page would have answered that question.

"I mean, thank you, Mister..."

"Vaughn," he said. "Wilder Vaughn. You can just call me Wild."

Jasmine nodded and gave him a small smile. "You can call me Jaz." Awkward silence followed until she broke it. "Does your personality live up to your name?"

♦♦♦♦

The question wasn't new to Wild, but the way she'd asked it was. Like the idea that he might be a little bit crazy both intrigued and frightened her. Usually comments of the sort had come from high school teachers or previous employers. A time or two it had come with a warning from a date's father, but never from someone interviewing for a job in *his* gym.

"Depends," he answered honestly. "If by wild, you mean fun, then yes. And between the two of us"—he gestured to Maddox—"I'm definitely the funner one." He was sure the comment would've earned him a solid punch to the arm if a prospective employee weren't sitting across from them.

"'Funner' isn't a word," Maddox corrected.

Wild rolled his eyes at Maddox, which made him laugh. That always did. Sometimes a raised eyebrow would follow when Maddox caught Wilder talking excitedly about getting matching Hawaiian shirts and tickets to Jimmy Buffett or stumbled around crashing into furniture in their apartment because he'd had too much tequila at Max's Public House after work...or starting demolition on their gym because his business partner hadn't yet hired the contractor they'd agreed on.

Mad's words always said *Stop, you're acting like a fool,* or something of the sort, but his eyes said something entirely different. They settled somewhere between *What am I gonna do with you?* and *I'm only intervening because I care.* That usually made Wild that much more eager to do whatever it was he'd been up to because he didn't want to offset the delicate balance of their friendship—a balance each man contributed to. Maddox would never let Wild do anything...well, too wild. And Wilder would never let Maddox become so serious about life that he wouldn't enjoy living it. Wild hoped, at least.

"I'm more fun, then," Wilder said. "And also more ambitious. If I had it my way, I would've expanded the gym and hired someone like you months ago," he said to Jasmine.

Now Maddox rolled *his* eyes. "*Ambitious* is one way to put it. Though I'd probably go with *crazy*."

There was something Jaz liked about the way the men looked at each other—like there was a trust and camaraderie between them that she hadn't experienced with another person. The realization saddened her a bit, but she wouldn't let it show. Witnessing it—though she wasn't a *part* of it—was still somehow satisfying. "Mad and Wild," she said. "Cute."

Maddox raised a dark eyebrow at her. "Did you just call us cute?"

It probably wasn't the most professional moment of Jasmine's life, but it certainly wasn't the most *un*professional one either. Though she wasn't sure that realization justified the remark. "Is that bad? If it helps, I meant it as a compliment."

She hadn't noticed Maddox's smooth, tan skin and pink lips before, but they now did things to her that she'd rather not be thinking about during an interview. She wondered what his ethnicity was, because she couldn't put her finger on it. Not that it mattered. Biology—and the gym—had been good to him.

That was for sure.

"That's how *I* took it," Wild said, drawing her attention back to him.

She was sure these guys had never been called cute in an interview before today, and the fact that she'd been the one to break that streak made her blush a bit, though she hoped they didn't notice.

"We're looking for someone who can teach a variety of group classes, Ms. Pritchett," Maddox said.

"Please. Jaz."

"Jaz," Maddox repeated, his tone no-nonsense, and the look he gave her was intense. "We already have someone for kickboxing, spin, and Zumba. We were thinking of adding some yoga or Pilates, possibly something else, though we aren't sure what yet. Guess it depends on what the new instructor's qualified to do. We're in the process of renovating the space currently, and we'd like to expand the variety of what we offer and, in turn, expand our clientele. I see you've taught yoga and have a few other certifications. Why don't you tell us a little bit about what you're willing to teach?"

Anything that pays the bills was what Jaz wanted to say, but she went with, "Yoga, for sure. I've taught it for a few years and have recently begun incorporating essential oils into my classes. But I can do Pilates, BODYPUMP, whatever you need really. I'm a Jaz of all trades." She hoped that her pun—and the bright smile she beamed at them—would lessen a little of the tension she felt when Maddox spoke. Wilder hadn't been kidding. His business partner was definitely the more serious one.

Maddox opened his mouth like he was about to reply, but Wilder spoke first. "How'd you like to be on the Transform team, Jaz?"

"You're hiring me?" She couldn't disguise the excitement in her voice, and she didn't want to.

Wild raised an eyebrow at his friend, most likely a silent plea for confirmation that his offer was an acceptable one.

After a long moment, Maddox extended his hand to her. "You're hired," he said sternly but added a nod and a small smile. "You have time for a tour?"

Jasmine took his large hand in hers and gave Maddox a nod of her own, thinking she had time for whatever these men had in store for her.

CHAPTER THREE

Wild and Mad shuffled into their apartment later than usual, which was impressive since they both always stayed until eleven on Wednesdays, when Transform closed. But after they walked around the gym and made sure everything was in its place before getting out of the cleaning crew's way, they went into the new section to see how things were coming along before taking care of the business side of things. They were happy with the progress so far on the renovation and managed to get started on the paperwork Jaz had filled out.

"I still can't believe you hired her on the spot," Maddox grumbled as he flopped down on their dark-brown sectional.

Wilder felt his forehead scrunch up as he kicked back in the recliner. "Why? That's exactly the kind of thing I'd do."

Mad grunted what Wild interpreted as "Good point."

"She's a good fit," Wild added, feeling the need to explain himself, though he wasn't sure why.

Mad laughed as he turned on the TV and flipped to a baseball game. "How do you figure?"

Wild sat up a little. "You don't think she is?"

"Not what I said. I just want to know why *you* think she is."

Wild sat back again, resisting the urge to huff. He hated when Mad did this shit. Imply something but then argue it wasn't what he said. "And I want to know why you think she isn't."

"I just told you, I didn't say—"

"Stop right there and cut the shit. Just tell me."

Maddox rubbed a hand over his eyes. He looked exhausted. Wild wondered if he was having trouble sleeping again or if it was simply from the long hours they'd been pulling. "She has next to no experience."

"Ya gotta start somewhere," Wild interjected.

Mad stared at him before he continued. "And you didn't even check the few references she did have. What if they're bullshit?"

"I don't remember you having a ton of references when I got you a job at the gym I was working at. And neither of us had any experience running a business when we decided to open ours."

"At least we'd worked in one," Mad mumbled.

"I got a good feeling about her, okay?"

Mad looked over at him, and their eyes stayed locked on one another for a moment before Mad nodded. "Okay."

For normal people, this would be a shit reason to hire someone. But for Mad and Wild, it was enough. Wild seemed to have a sixth sense when it came to people, and his instincts were rarely wrong. Not to mention he'd only given someone a chance like this based on a good feeling once before. And that had worked out pretty well for the both of them.

Maddox groaned and got up from the couch. "I'm going to bed. You want this on?" he asked, gesturing toward the TV.

"Nah, I'm going to bed too."

"Okay. See you in the morning."

"I'll be here."

It was a familiar response, but one that was more promise than trite send-off. Wild sat there for a few more minutes, gearing himself up to move. Finally, he pushed himself out of the recliner and walked to his room to retrieve his towel. He faintly heard water running in Maddox's room as he passed, since he had the master with its own bathroom. Grabbing what he needed, Wild made his way into the hall bathroom and turned the water on as hot as he'd be able to stand. He let the room steam up a bit as he brushed his teeth. He caught a glimpse of himself in the mirror and thought about how fucking tired he looked. While he was excited about the changes at the gym, it was also exhausting work.

A few moments later, he stepped into the shower and under the hot spray. He hung his head and watched the water run down the ridges of his abdomen. Some might have called him vain, but Wild liked how he looked. He worked damn hard on his physique. Every vein had been hard-earned in the gym, and every ab had been cut by following a strict nutrition plan. That was what he loved about fitness: there were no limits to what someone could achieve as long as they were willing to work for it.

Taking a deep breath, he raised his face into the stream of water before stepping back and grabbing the soap. He began lazily running it over his body, watching the water rinse the suds away. The more he ran his hands over himself, the more his body tingled with the touch and the harder his dick became. He'd been so consumed with the renovations, it'd been a while since he'd gotten laid—something he'd have to rectify if touching his own body was turning him on.

Once he was done with the soap, he took his cock in his hand and slowly dragged his fist over the steely flesh, twisting his wrist a bit at the flared head. His hold was relaxed as he enjoyed the sensation with no desire to rush to the finish line. Putting his other hand on the wall, he leaned forward, the water running down his back as he dragged his fist up and down his length. For the first time that day, his mind was blank, and all he could think was how good it felt to touch himself. Soon, his hips started to thrust a bit, his body deciding it was done with slow and his need to get off becoming more urgent.

Wilder picked up the pace, his hand flying more quickly over his cock as his hips continued to buck as if he was pushing into the tight pussy of a woman. His balls were full, and tingles were zinging up and down his spine. The water dripping down on his cock was an added stimulation that ramped him up even more. He straightened as his climax began to barrel down on him, the heat of the moment causing a montage of beautiful women to float across his mental movie screen as he imagined emptying himself into any one of them. How great that would feel. How much pleasure he'd find as he buried his cock inside them. Then, a certain face sprang to mind and captured his focus. Smooth dark hair hung over her shoulders, and deep green eyes closed slowly in front of him. Somehow, she'd made her way into his brain—or more than his brain, it seemed. His entire body felt her presence so completely he could barely process all of it before he was coming—grunting his relief as his entire body spasmed in on itself. With the exertion of coming so hard, his shoulders bowed forward as he continued to milk his dick with his hand.

When the last of his come pulsed through his slit, Wilder opened his eyes in time to watch the water wash it away. All evidence of his orgasm gone, just as he hoped the knowledge that he'd blown his load to the image of Jaz would wash away as well.

CHAPTER FOUR

Jasmine finished putting her belongings in the women's locker room and then headed out to the gym where Maddox had told her to meet him. She found him standing near the barbell rack, laughing with a guy squatting a weight she was shocked he could lift because he was about a foot and a half shorter and clearly a lot lighter than Maddox. At her approach, both men turned toward her, and Maddox smiled. He seemed more jovial than he'd been when she'd first met him, and she attributed it to the fact that he probably liked the training part of his job much more than the managerial side.

"Jaz, this is Bull. He practically lives here," Maddox said. "Bull, Jasmine Pritchett. She's one of the new trainers we hired. She'll be teaching some yoga and a few other classes in the new space."

"Pleasure to meet you."

She wanted to ask about his nickname, but judging from the amount of weight he was lifting, she could guess. He looked to be about her mom's age, and she found herself glad that her mother would probably never meet him. Despite Bull's small stature, he was classically good-looking, with a square jaw, salt-and-pepper hair, and broad shoulders.

Bull wiped his hand on his shorts before shaking Jasmine's

hand, and she appreciated the courtesy, even though it wasn't necessary. A little sweat didn't bother her.

"Welcome," Bull said. Then he lifted his damp navy T-shirt up to his face to absorb the moisture before handing a fifteen-pound weight to Maddox to put on the barbell. "I probably won't be taking any of your classes anytime soon, but it's good to have a new face around here. Especially one that's prettier to look at than your two bosses'."

The comment made Jaz laugh. It might've seemed creepy coming from someone else, but Bull had a warm innocence to him that made the remark more of a compliment than it otherwise might have been. Still, it earned him a swat to the arm and a "Watch it" from Maddox.

His eyes seemed to warn Bull as much as his words did, indicating to her that Maddox cared more about Bull saying something inappropriate than about insulting him and Wild. She appreciated it but didn't really need it.

Jaz had learned to handle just about any situation at an early age out of necessity. No one else had been there to do it for her. She'd worked since she was fourteen, and since most of her jobs resulted in her being surrounded by men, she had learned when and how to put them in their place. She'd learned more about sex during her shifts at the local pizza place than she had from her middle school health classes, and though she didn't mind the vulgar language—as long as it wasn't directed at her—she didn't hesitate to speak up if a conversation bordered on offensive.

Maddox told Bull they'd see him in a bit, and then he let Jaz know that Wild was running a little late but would be here soon so she could shadow him. Though her job didn't require her to conduct one-on-one personal training sessions with people—at least, not yet—Maddox and Wilder thought she would benefit from more of a hands-on tour of the facility and its day-to-day operations than the quick overview they'd given her the day she'd been hired.

Since her studio space wasn't quite ready, she had no objections to shadowing the men until it was ready. Not only would she get paid sooner, she liked the idea of spending more time with Maddox and Wilder so she could get to know them.

Maddox showed her how to use the computer to clock in and out and sign in clients when they arrived, as well as adjust the trainers' schedules if needed. "Everyone knows all of this, and we just hired someone to help out at the front desk," he explained. "I'm not showing you because I expect you to be our secretary."

He seemed more concerned about the comment than he should've been, and she wanted to tell him she didn't take offense to it, but he continued before she could speak. "We could also use some help coming up with the best way to have clients book group classes. We don't want them getting too crowded, but we don't want people signing up to save a spot only to cancel at the last minute either."

She told him she'd give it some thought and do a little research over the next few days.

Their conversation was interrupted by an excited Wilder pulling open the glass door and yelling that he had coffee.

Jasmine eagerly accepted the cup.

"Cream and sugar are in the bag," he said, offering it to her.

"Black's good for me, actually."

"See?" Maddox said, taking one of the other two cups. "Some people know how to drink coffee the right way."

Wild was already dumping in sugar packets and creamers, stirring the liquid every so often and evaluating the color and taste.

Maddox and Jaz exchanged disgusted glances before Mad leaned in and whispered, "I'm sorry you need to witness the desecration of such a fine beverage."

"Me too," she whispered back before taking a sip of her coffee. "That's not exactly the healthiest thing to be putting in your body either."

Wilder held his arms out and looked down at himself before raising his head back up at her. "You saying I need to change how I look?" he teased with a smile that was complete with those dimples she'd noticed the previous week when she interviewed.

She was definitely *not* saying he should change his appearance. He was in a tighter shirt than he'd been in last time—black Dri-FIT with no sleeves—so she could see the definition of his abs and his perfectly defined shoulders and biceps. His orange-and-gray shorts came a little above his knees and fit perfectly, allowing a view of the bottom of his quad muscle. It made her want to see higher. "Not what I said at all. I was actually wondering the opposite. How do you look like"—she moved her hand up and down the space in front of his body—"*that,* if you put all that shit in one cup of coffee?"

"My one and only weakness, I suppose. Like Kryptonite to Superman," Wild explained, causing Maddox to roll his eyes. "I only have one cup of coffee a day, and then it's back to boring shit like chicken and rice the rest of the time."

"I try to keep Wilder from providing nutritional counseling to the clients as much as possible," Mad interjected. "He has the metabolism of a teenager and the appetite of a ravenous lion. He could probably eat a lot worse than he does and still look good."

"That's why it's so impressive that I can stick to such a healthy diet," Wild said.

"Do you do a lot of that here?" Jaz asked. She was actually pretty strict about what she ate as well, though it was likely she was laxer about it than Wilder. Overall, she did enjoy eating well, like the discipline of it all—that she had control over what she put into her body, what it looked like, and how it functioned. She felt better when she fueled her body with nutritious foods, and it had the added benefit of helping her *look* better as well. That said, she was a big fan of using her cheat days. "Like nutritional counseling? Or workshops or anything?"

"Some," Mad answered. "Mostly on an as-needed one-on-one basis. We've never done anything too formal." He looked at Wild and then back to Jaz. "Okay, well, I hate to leave you in the hands of my lesser half, but I have to get going. I have an appointment at the bathroom place to pick out the fixtures and stuff for the new space." He explained that because some of the clients they'd be getting for their yoga and studio classes might not want to walk through the more industrial main space to use the bathroom because guys dropped barbells and some of the women squatted close to double their own weight up, they decided to install some in the new part of the gym. "It'll just be two unisex bathrooms, each with a shower, toilet, and sink. But it'll feel like a separate space if people want to treat it that way."

It was a great idea since, from what the guys had told her, the new gym space would have a much more upscale feel. "Sounds good. I'll see you later, then," she said.

Maddox said goodbye and left Wild with, "Don't do anything to make our new hire quit on her first day."

"Wouldn't dream of it," Wild said with a smile.

Jaz wondered if the comment had been a joke or a warning based on a prior situation, but she didn't think it was her place to ask. And it didn't matter anyway. It would take a lot to make her leave a good job with two hot bosses who also seemed pretty damn cool.

♦♦♦♦

Maddox's appointment had taken almost three hours, which was two hours longer than he'd anticipated. He'd had to decide on the bathroom layouts, and they'd tried to upsell him on fixtures and tiles that were unnecessary. They'd almost convinced him that it would be more economical—though somehow still more expensive—to create one men's room with two stalls and a shower and one women's room with the same. The extra toilets didn't add much to the cost, and ultimately, it gave people the ability to use the bathroom even if someone was using the shower. It had seemed like a good idea until he figured if they had to pee that bad they could just use the bathroom in the other part of the gym if both in the new space were occupied. So after two hours of debating which would be best, he went with his gut and decided on his original plan. He wished he'd trusted himself more because his instincts didn't usually mislead him.

After he left, he stopped at a new restaurant to grab something for lunch and then headed back to the gym so he could show the bathroom choices to Wild. He didn't plan on making any major changes, and most likely Wild wouldn't have any objections to what he'd picked—which were mostly white and gray like they'd talked about. Wilder knew how indecisive he could be, so he'd asked Mad if he'd go without him, and Maddox was happy to do so. Wilder would've been there all day choosing between stainless steel and brushed nickel and sitting on toilets to feel their level of comfort. Maddox didn't mind being the decision guy.

When he didn't see Wild or Jaz in the gym, he figured they must've gone to the place on the corner to grab something to eat. Mad assumed they'd be back soon since both men had an agreement not to leave the gym for an extended period of time if the other was out. Keith, a trainer who'd worked there for over a year, was working that day as well, so it wasn't like Wild had left the place unattended. And midday was usually their slowest time. Still, they thought it was best to have one of the owners present at all times if possible.

Maddox settled into the desk at the front to check the gym's email and update their website with the new classes they'd be offering soon—something he'd been meaning to do since they'd hired Jaz and another trainer, Thad, but hadn't gotten around to—when he heard banging coming from the construction space. The contractor had told him that he and his crew had to finish another job today and they'd be back tomorrow, but Maddox was happy they must have completed it early and decided to come here once they were done.

Until he realized the possibility that the contractor and his guys weren't the ones working in there. He looked to Bull, one of the only clients in the gym. When he averted his eyes from Mad's gaze, Maddox knew he had the answer.

Within seconds, Maddox was entering the new gym space. He didn't see anyone at first, so he went down the hall to the back room. And that was when his greatest fear was confirmed: the woman they'd hired to teach fitness classes was currently kneeling, hammering pieces of laminate wood flooring into place while his nutjob of a business partner was standing over a table saw, cutting floorboards.

Mad stared silently for a moment because he was worried that if he startled either one of them, the situation might become more dangerous than it already was. Which, in his determination, was like a seven or eight on the scale of Safe to Imminent Death.

A few seconds later, the saw stopped, and Wild turned, looking like a spiky-haired fucking fly in his safety goggles. "Oh, hey. When did you get back? Everything go okay?"

"Are you seriously asking *me* questions right now? What the fuck are you doing?"

"Finishing the floor," Wild answered simply.

Mad rubbed a hand over his face in frustration and let out a deep sigh. "You don't know how to put in a floor," he said. "And you can't use George's equipment. That's a liability."

"For *them*," Wilder corrected. "It's not like we can be sued for using the gigantic saw they left in our building. And also, I obviously do know how to put a floor in." He gestured to their progress, which was about three-quarters of the way done. To Mad's knowledge, the men hadn't even begun the flooring in that room yet. "Why wait for the contractor when it's something we can do ourselves?"

This fucker. "Uh, because we're paying him and you're going to kill yourself and our new employee. You're supposed to be letting Jaz shadow you, not subjecting her to hard labor." At the mention of Jaz's name, he looked down at her. She was still kneeling, hammer and rubber block in hand, looking up at the two men.

"It was actually my fault," Jaz said. "Wild was telling me the studio spaces wouldn't be done for another week or two because the contractor was already behind and was on another job today. I joked that we should just finish it ourselves. I'm sorry."

Mad sighed again and ran a hand through his short, dark hair. He didn't want Jaz to think he was reprimanding her, and despite the fact that she took the blame, Mad had a hard time believing it was her fault. "It's okay. You guys actually did a pretty good job," he admitted. "I just don't want you getting hurt."

Jaz looked relieved, and he realized she probably thought her new job might have been in jeopardy. "Teaching Wild to use the saw was definitely the most dangerous part. I offered to do the cutting, but he wouldn't let me."

What a gentleman. Apparently the man at least had *some* common sense, though. "Where did you learn to do this?"

"I helped one of my stepdads replace our kitchen floor once."

Maddox wondered just how many stepdads she'd had, but it obviously wasn't his place to ask.

"So we good now?" Wild asked, holding another floorboard he'd just measured and marked.

"Yeah," Maddox conceded. "Let me go finish my lunch, and then I'll give you guys a hand."

"That's what's up," Wild said, extending his gloved hand to Maddox for a fist bump, which Mad happily gave him.

What the hell was he gonna do with these two?

CHAPTER FIVE

"You takin' off for the night?" Wild asked when he saw Jasmine coming out of the locker room with her backpack slung over her shoulder.

She'd been taking a sip from her steel water bottle but pulled it away from her mouth and swallowed. Wild tried not to stare at the way her throat worked as the water slid down it. "I was going to. Mad said I could head out. Did you need me to stay?"

Wild felt bad he'd asked if she was leaving, because he had no intention of asking her to stay, and that was clearly what she thought. "No. No, you're good. I'm good." And for some stupid-ass reason, he added, "We're good."

She smiled but kept her lips tight like she was trying like hell to suppress a laugh. "Good," she said, making Wilder the first one to laugh.

"What *is* that?" he asked, pointing to the symbol on the inside of her upper arm when she lifted it to take another sip of water. He'd been looking at the tattoo since she started three days ago and hadn't asked, though he'd been wondering. It was a bunch of spirals that looked similar to an infinity symbol, but he knew it wasn't one. How the fuck did you google symbols if you didn't know the name?

"It's called an unalome." She held out her arm and pointed to where it began closer to her elbow. "The wider spirals symbolize struggles in life. They get thinner as it goes because it's supposed to represent the path to enlightenment."

"Oh, so you're trying to become enlightened? Is that like...a yoga thing or something?"

She laughed again. "It's more like a human thing, I guess. And no, I'm definitely not enlightened. I don't even know if someone can truly become that way."

This woman perplexed him. "Then why do you have it?"

Giving him a shrug, she traced a thumb over the lines on her arm up to the top. "Guess I figure trying is better than nothing. I've never been any good at quitting."

Wild nodded slowly. He wasn't one to philosophize, but even he had to admit that made sense. He'd basically told Maddox a version of that same truth from time to time over the years. "Well, if there's one thing you'd wanna suck at, quitting's a pretty good choice. Makes me feel better about our decision to hire you."

"You didn't feel good about it already?"

"No. Yes. I mean, no, that's not what I meant." When did he turn into a bumbling idiot? "I just meant hopefully it means you'll be sticking around for a while. This industry has a pretty high turnover rate."

"Well, I don't plan on going anywhere, so I guess you guys are stuck with me for a while."

"Guess we are," Wild said. And he couldn't have been happier.

♦♦♦♦

Jasmine had established herself at Transform quickly and was wrapping up what she'd call a successful first few days. Mad and Wild were the first bosses she'd ever actually *liked.* She'd had some she tolerated, but she couldn't really say she'd ever enjoyed a boss's company before. Not until now, at least. It made her even happier she'd moved away from home.

Pulling her other backpack strap over her shoulder, she waved goodbye to Maddox and headed toward the bus stop a block away. Since she'd moved here, she hadn't gone anywhere on public transit besides work and her apartment, and she wondered what other places it might take her.

Jasmine thought back to when she was a kid, when she and her neighbor Maggie would hop on random buses and take them into the city. It hadn't ever occurred to her that such a decision could be a dangerous one, and she thought about how lucky they'd been to have never been kidnapped or mugged...or worse. They were only about twelve when their bus adventures had come to an abrupt end. They had run toward the back of the bus as they always had, but when they got there, they found a man in a top hat masturbating to a *Wonder Woman* comic book.

Though that situation had ended without incident, it had been one of her first introductions to how fucked up the world could be. Somehow, over the course of the next decade or so, she'd become desensitized to weirdos. They were as much a part of the world as anyone else, and as long as they weren't harming anyone, they deserved to live in it too. Though the top hat *had* been a tad much.

But now, as she sat on the bench in the bus shelter, waiting for the 308 to take her back to her little studio that still didn't have a box spring for her mattress, her weirdo alarm was howling.

"Can you move over a bit?" she asked the man who'd sat down only an inch or so from her. She wasn't sure why she didn't just stand, but she identified that mistake immediately when instead of moving away from her, he moved closer. So close, his leg touched hers.

"Other way," she said dryly. It wasn't like she was unaccustomed to guys hitting on her.

"I like it *here*," he said, putting a hand on her leg, which she shoved away before jumping up from the bench.

Wanting nothing more than to distance herself from the man, Jaz headed back to the gym, thinking her first big purchase would need to be a car. Her old Jetta had been kind enough to complete the move here but had died soon after.

Jasmine liked to think she was capable of taking care of herself. And she was. In most situations, anyway. But she wasn't naïve enough to think she could fight off a large man if it came to that. It was a weakness she hoped to rectify by taking a self-defense class if she ever had the time or money.

"What'd you forget?" Maddox asked when she opened the door to the gym again.

"Oh. Nothing, actually. I'm just gonna call an Uber."

"Did the bus come already?" He looked at his watch.

"Nah," she said, hoping to sound more casual than she felt. "There's some gross dude out there, so I'm treating myself to a chauffeur tonight."

"Gross how?" Maddox asked.

She sensed a change in his demeanor almost immediately. His eyebrows pressed together, and she could've sworn she saw the veins in his neck and arms expand.

"Just sitting too close to me. It's no big deal. I'm used to it."

Maddox stared at her before asking, "Did he touch you?"

She wasn't sure how to answer because she had a feeling no matter what she said, Maddox's reaction would be the same. "Just sat close to me, and when I asked him to move, he moved closer."

"So is that a yes or no?"

"I mean, just his side touched mine. Then when I asked him to move, he put a hand on my leg."

Mad's jaw locked, and his face grew darker.

"It's fine. I'll call an Uber," she said. But before she'd finished her sentence, Maddox was out the door. He didn't *run* to the bus stop. It was more of an angry march—one that included clenched fists she didn't know if he was planning to use.

She couldn't hear what Mad said when he got there, but she saw him grab the guy by the collar and pull him toward himself. After a few moments, Maddox let go, shoving the guy back down on the bench. But he didn't last there long. He was up in an instant and heading the opposite way down the sidewalk, pulling his hood over his head and shoving his hands in his pockets. He looked like a dog with its tail between its legs. Though the man at the bus stop was large, Maddox was larger—and he somehow looked even bigger than usual, as if his size increased in proportion to his anger. It was like watching the Incredible Hulk threaten a mouse. It was one of the hottest things anyone had ever done for her.

"What did you say to him?" Jaz asked when Maddox returned.

"He won't be back again," was all Mad said. "Come on, I'll drive you."

Jaz wasn't sure what to say at first. No one had ever stood up for her like that before. She didn't know if it was because typically she could stand up for herself or if she wasn't the type of person who got herself into situations that required people to step in and help, but she was appreciative nonetheless. "Thanks, Mad. You don't have to do that, though. You have to close up."

"Wild has another PT client. He can close. Let's go."

Something told her not to argue. Maddox wasn't going to take no for an answer, so she didn't say it. She simply nodded a grateful *okay* and wondered why the hell he'd reacted like he had on behalf of someone he barely knew.

CHAPTER SIX

As he drove the two miles or so to Jasmine's apartment, Maddox told himself he'd gone a bit too far. The guy had been a little strange, and though touching Jasmine had been inappropriate, the man hadn't hurt her. But Maddox knew things like that could escalate quickly. And the idea of someone putting their hands on her without her permission made him see red.

"It's nice of you to drive me home," she said. "You really didn't have to."

"Anytime," Maddox replied, and he meant it. "There are some strange people in the city, but typically it's a good area. Promise."

"It's all right. I don't come from the nicest area myself, so sadly I'm used to creeps and society's rejects." She laughed after she said it, but her words rang true nonetheless.

Maddox had looked at her résumé, but it didn't reveal much about her past other than work history. "Where'd you grow up?"

She'd been looking out the window as the glow of stores and streetlights blurred by them, but she shifted her attention to him before she spoke. "A little suburb outside of Wilmington, but I moved right after high school. Just kind of bounced around. I know that sounds pretty bad, but I swear I'm more stable than that makes me seem."

"No judgment on my part," Maddox said. "I joined the army my junior year of high school. The fact that I chose to do boot camp that summer instead of go to the beach and party like all my friends should tell you what I thought of my life."

"You were in the army? Reserves or active duty?"

"Active duty," was all he said, and the hardness to his voice must've told Jasmine to leave it there because she didn't say anything more. The truck was too quiet for Maddox, and he felt the need to fill the silence. "You have any brothers or sisters?"

"Two sisters. Isabella's three years older and Ariel's two years younger."

"I don't think I've ever known anyone named Ariel," Maddox said.

"I'm not surprised." Jasmine laughed and pulled the hair tie out of her hair. She ran her fingers through the dark strands, and Maddox found himself more drawn to the action than he wanted to admit. "It takes a special kind of person to name her kids after Disney princesses."

"Oh my God, I never would've even noticed that." He knew Ariel from *The Little Mermaid,* but it took him a little longer to remember what movie the name Jasmine was from. "What's Isabella from?"

"*Beauty and the Beast.* My mom always called her Belle for short, but after Isabella saw the movie for the first time, she insisted we all call her by her full name. She hated that she was named after a girl who fell in love with her captor."

"Can't say I blame her," Maddox said. "The princess idea

is pretty cool, though."

"More like cruel. We didn't exactly live a royal lifestyle, and it was like the universe was constantly reminding us that we weren't supposed to be in our own skin or something. My mom still calls Isabella 'Belle.' It drives my sister crazy, but our mom means well, so we tolerate all the strange stuff she does." She laughed, but it sounded forced.

Maddox wondered what exactly Jaz's upbringing had been like, but he didn't think he was in a place to ask after only knowing her a few days. Jasmine showed him where her apartment building was, and he pulled up in front, putting on the hazards when he stopped. "I'd walk you up, but I'm double-parked."

"I think I can make it to the door on my own. Thanks, though. And I appreciate the ride."

Maddox nodded, assuring her again that a ride was a standing offer if she ever needed one. "I'll see you tomorrow?" he asked, leaning on the gear shift as he looked at Jaz through the open window.

"Bright and early," she said with a smile.

Maddox watched her walk to the door of her building, wondering why the hell he couldn't take his eyes off her.

♦ ♦ ♦ ♦

Once inside her apartment, Jasmine plopped down on a chair and began flipping through her mail. It definitely never took long to start receiving bills at a new place, that was for sure. She tossed them on the coffee table, not even bothering to open them before she got her first paycheck. The only thing left was an envelope from her mom's address. She smiled, thinking how sweet it was for her mom to send her a card already. No matter where Jaz ended up, her mom always sent a note or a card shortly after she settled in.

Had Jaz known it was an invitation to her mother's wedding, she wouldn't have even opened the envelope. But there it was:

Please celebrate the marriage of Anna Mathers and Jethro Busch on the seventeenth of October. More details to come.

Then, at the bottom, as a kind of personal touch, her mom had written:

Hope you can make it :)

Jaz shut her eyes as if the inability to see what she'd just read would somehow make it less true. Her mom still had Greg's last name, and here she was already sending out an invitation to what would be her fifth wedding...to this...Jethro guy. For all Jasmine knew, her mom was still paying off her third wedding, which she'd spent about twenty grand on because she insisted that Pete was "the one." Nothing like having your fourth husband help to pay off the debt from your marriage to your third. Anna Pritchett/Williams/Scott/Mathers/soon-to-be-Busch was an interesting woman.

Against her logical judgment, Jasmine picked up the phone. "I'm definitely not getting you a present this time," Jaz said when her mom answered.

"Oh good! That means you're coming! And I'm glad it made it there."

"Why wouldn't it make it here? And more importantly, why am I getting an invitation to *another* one of your weddings?"

"You're my daughter, Jasmine. It would be rude for me not to invite you. And anyway, it's a save-the-date. The invitation probably won't come for another month or so. We still need to pick them out."

"Is the place giving you a discount this time since you're a frequent customer?"

"Very funny," her mom said. "I'm hoping you girls will be in the wedding."

Jasmine laughed. "I wouldn't want to ruin our streak."

"Why can't you just be happy for me?" Her mom didn't sound nearly as hurt as the words led her to seem.

"Because I'm still working on being happy for you and your last marriage. Which was only like...a year ago. You still have Greg's last name, Mom."

"Well, it's pointless to change it back to Pritchett when it'll be Busch soon anyway."

Even Jasmine could admit that it was a valid point, but her mom should probably just consider not changing it from Pritchett at all. Jasmine would never say that out loud, though, so she sighed instead. But she knew her mom probably recognized it for what it was: a nonverbal concession of sorts. Her mom would always be a serial wife. Anna Pritchett jumped from one relationship to the next, though to Jasmine's knowledge, her mother had never actually been unfaithful. It was more that she got bored—or maybe disinterested would be more accurate. What excited her initially about a person—

what she fell in love with—eventually wouldn't hold the same intrigue it once had. It was like watching the sun rise and fall. And when the appeal faded, her mother's love seemed to fade with it until eventually it dissolved completely.

It was a vicious cycle but one that Anna seemed so okay with she almost embraced it. And that was something Jasmine never thought she would be able to understand. Jaz tried to tell her mom that the novelty of a relationship wearing off didn't mean that the relationship itself needed to fall apart, but since Jaz hadn't even had what her mom considered a "steady boyfriend," Jasmine's opinion was basically the equivalent of a kindergartner's.

"So how's your new place?" Anna asked, causing Jasmine to look at her surrounding apartment. It didn't have much furniture to speak of because before she moved here, she'd donated much of her old furniture in lieu of moving it. She figured the move would be cheaper that way, and she could use the money she saved to buy some new stuff. That would be another plan that would have to come to fruition once she got an actual paycheck. For the moment, her priority was getting a car.

"It's nice. Still getting settled in. I should probably get some more things unpacked," she said. "It's getting late."

"It's a quarter to nine."

"I've been up since four thirty."

Her mom gasped in a way that was much too excessive for the situation. "That's an ungodly hour, Jasmine."

Jasmine smiled, thinking that she agreed but would happily do it the next day. So far, she loved her job at Transform, and she was just getting started. Sure, the hours could be long, but not only would the money be worth it, she had a feeling the friendships would be too. “It is. I do much better going to bed at that time than I do getting up. Although I don’t technically have a *bed* yet,” she said, thinking of the mattress on the floor of the bedroom.

“Oh my God, honey. I hate thinking of you in a strange place without a bed. You know you can come home.”

Jasmine sighed, but her heart warmed at the offer she knew she’d never take. It was important for her to make her own way in the world, no matter how difficult it would be. She didn’t want to have to depend on anyone but herself, and she looked forward to finally being able to grow roots somewhere. “I know. I’m fine. Really. I’ll call you next week?”

“Okay, I’ll talk to you then. Good luck getting settled.”

“Thanks. And Mom?” she said. “Of course I’ll be a bridesmaid.”

Her mom was silent for a moment, and Jaz suspected she was crying. “Thank you. That means a lot to me.”

Jasmine knew it did even before she said it. It was the reason she wouldn’t miss being part of her mom’s wedding. No matter how many there might be.

CHAPTER SEVEN

"Here's to finally finishing the renovation from hell!" Wilder yelled to the corner of the bar they'd commandeered about thirty minutes ago. He couldn't deny it. He was relieved to have everything finished. Despite his insistence on getting the gym where they wanted it, he had also worried it'd be a disaster, which would've resulted in Mad never letting Wild make any business decisions ever again.

Okay, maybe that was a slight exaggeration, but he definitely would've given Wild a hard time for the foreseeable future, and who had time for that shit? Wild raised his beer glass higher. "And to all our new hires. Thanks for boarding the crazy train."

Hoots and hollers erupted all around. Thank God they knew the owner of the bar, and Wild could be fairly confident they wouldn't get tossed out for being too rowdy. "Speech!" Dan, one of the experienced trainers, yelled.

"From me?" Wild asked, but he continued before receiving an answer. "All right. It all started when I was a boy—"

"Not you, you asshole." Dan laughed. "The newbies."

Wild looked around at everyone. "Oh. Yeah, okay, that makes more sense. Have at it, guys."

Jaz, a young guy named Thad who they'd gotten to teach

kickboxing, and a new woman named Yohanna who'd just graduated from college and would be helping out at the front desk all looked at one another with wide eyes and alarm written clearly across their faces. After a few seconds of a discussion held completely with their eyes, Jaz spoke up.

"Okay. I'll say...something. Thanks for this awkward moment, Dan."

Dan smiled, looking pleased with himself.

Jaz stood, looking great in a white racerback tank and black tights. Not that Wild was thinking about how she looked or anything.

"It's been great getting to know everyone and getting to be part of this certifiably insane group of people."

Everyone laughed at her words, and Craig, another trainer, yelled, "Hell yeah!"

Jaz smiled widely, the only way Wild had ever seen her smile. She was one of those people who always smiled with her entire being, and it made Wild's own lips quirk up at the corners.

"So thanks to Wilder and Maddox for giving me a chance to work at a great facility with a great group of people." She held her glass up, and they all followed suit.

When they were done, all eyes turned to Thad, who stood up halfway before saying, "Yeah, uh, what she said."

"Coward," Maddox yelled, which made Wild laugh. He looked over at Mad, who looked relaxed and happy, which Wild enjoyed seeing. Mad carried the weight of the world on his shoulders sometimes, and it was good to see him loosening up.

"I'm punking out too," Yohanna announced.

"You're all lame. Who the hell hired you?" Wild asked, bursting into laughter when they both glared at him.

The night progressed in raucous fashion, with people sharing stories about nightmare clients and gym mishaps.

"I have a good one," Jaz, who'd ended up sandwiched between Mad and Wild, said. "Maddox, remember that time you came in and Wild and I were installing the new floor? Ah, memories."

"That was only like a month ago," Mad grumbled.

Everyone burst out laughing. "I'm just teasing," Jaz said through her laughter. "Though your face was pretty epic."

"I thought you morons were going to cut your hands off and bleed all over my new flooring."

"Is it sad that I'm not sure which you would've been more upset by—us losing our hands or ruining your precious floor?" Wild joked.

"The fact that you have to ask shows how little you know me. It took me a month to pick out that wood."

"You're such a dick," Wild said with more affection than the words typically warranted.

Mad smirked as he lifted his beer bottle to his lips and took a swig. Wild couldn't help but return the smile. The stress of the past couple of months seemed to slough off him, leaving in its wake a steady thrum of contentment Wild wanted to bask in. He leaned back in his chair and watched the people around him, taking in their happy faces and the easy way they interacted. He'd helped create this. He and Mad.

He felt Jaz lean back in her chair as well, putting her

flesh up against his bicep. Tilting her head back, she said in a low voice, "You guys have built an incredible thing here, Wild Man."

Wilder felt warmth rush through him, both at her words and at the nickname she'd bestowed on him after the flooring incident. And maybe her proximity had a little to do with it as well. He took a deep breath before turning to look at her, their faces mere inches apart. "Yeah, we have. Thanks for helping us make it even better."

An adorable flush spread across her cheeks as she held his gaze. "You're welcome," she said softly.

They both smiled at one another before Jaz broke eye contact. Though Wilder noticed she stayed where she was, her arm firmly pressed against his. As far as he was concerned, the night couldn't get any more perfect.

♦♦♦♦

Based on the goofy grin Wild kept shooting everyone, Mad could tell he was drunk. He was also a touchy drunk, and Wild currently had his arm draped around Dan's neck while he rested his other hand on Thad's shoulder, telling them some story they'd most likely heard before.

"Get it?" Wild asked loudly. "The mom is also the sister."

Yup, completely wasted.

"Good luck getting him out of here," Jaz said as she plopped down on the chair next to him. She'd gotten up for a while to circulate, but Mad was glad she was back. There was something...comfortable about her. Maddox typically didn't like being stuck talking to people he didn't know well, but he enjoyed Jaz's company.

"It won't be so bad. He tires out quickly."

Jaz laughed at that. "Like a toddler?"

Maddox joined her in her laughter. "Exactly like that."

Taking a sip of her water, Jaz sat up straighter. "I want you to sit in on my first yoga class."

Maddox slowly panned his head so he was looking at her. "Does this frame look like it bends easily?"

"Not particularly," she said with a wide smile. "I think it'll be fun getting you all tied up like a pretzel. But that's not why I'm asking." She took another sip of her water before setting the glass down and turning her body completely toward him. "I don't have a ton of experience, which I know you know because you saw my résumé. But I want to be good at what I do. Really good. So I need someone to tell me what I can be doing to improve."

Maddox took in the earnestness in her expression and became even more impressed by her than he already had been. "I think having that attitude is already a step in the right direction," he said.

Jaz's answering eye roll told him that wasn't the answer she was looking for.

Mad tried again. "I think Wild would be better suited to..." The shaking of Jaz's head caused him to stop speaking.

"Wild is too nice," she explained.

"Gee thanks," Mad replied dryly.

"Shut up. You know what I mean. And please ignore that I just told you to shut up. That was inappropriate. Anyway, Wild will try to figure out the nicest way possible to tell me I suck.

And that doesn't do me any good. I need someone who will just come out with it, feelings be damned."

Maddox sat and digested her words for a second. He wasn't sure he liked being someone she thought didn't care about other people's feelings.

Something must've shown on his face, because she added, "I just think your feedback will be more constructive than his. I'm probably saying this all wrong, because I mean what I'm saying as a compliment. I trust you to tell me what I need to know to be the best I can be."

Her words hit a weak spot in his armor. There was a time when he'd been that guy for a whole unit of men. Then, for a long time, he'd only been that guy for Wilder. He tapped into it while training clients, but it wasn't the same. The trust they put in him didn't feel as heavy as the trust Jaz was putting in him. "You better not make me look like an asshole," he grumbled.

The bright smile that lit up her face made it impossible for him to hold on to his grumpy exterior. "You don't even have to participate if you really don't want to," she assured him.

He smiled back at her, feeling himself get a little lost in the moment, but thankfully not so much that he didn't notice Wilder rounding the table toward them. His drunk best friend threw an arm around each of them and leaned heavily. He really must've been plowed. Wild was usually good about not startling Mad from behind. If Maddox hadn't noticed him coming, his reaction likely would've needed some explaining. But as it was, he was able to relax under the weight of his friend. "Feeling good there, buddy?"

"So good. Tequila is the best," Wild declared.

"I'll remind you of that tomorrow morning."

"Oh, speaking of tomorrow," Jaz said. "Now that I have a car, I was thinking of driving out to Canyon Falls and hiking around there. Have you guys ever been? I wanted to know if it was worth the drive or not."

"Oh man, I haven't been there in forever," Wild said, his voice almost coming out like a whine, as if someone had told him Disney World had closed down.

"We were just there last summer."

"Like I said—forever."

Maddox shook his head and looked at Jaz. "It's great there. They have a bunch of trails to choose from, depending on your skill level, and the views are breathtaking. It's definitely worth the trip."

"We should go with her," Wild said to Maddox before turning to Jaz. "We should go with you. You'll have so much more fun with us there. And we're all off tomorrow. It was meant to be." It was less serendipitous than Wild was making it out to be. They both always had off Sundays, and since they didn't run any classes, there'd be no need for Jaz to be there either.

Jaz laughed. "You sure you're going to be up for it?"

Wild let out a "Pfft" and turned to Mad. "Does she know who she's talking to?"

"Clearly not," Maddox said.

Wild moved his hand from her shoulder and pointed to himself. "I am a hiking afician-aficio-afiscin—goddamnit, Mad tell her the word I mean."

"Aficionado?" Mad supplied.

Wilder nodded. “That. I’m that.”

“Good to know,” Jaz replied, still looking skeptical.

“He’ll be fine. He typically bounces back from nights like this pretty quickly.”

“In that case, I’d love the company,” Jaz said.

“You sure?” Maddox asked. “I don’t want to intrude on your personal time.”

“No way. I’m a social creature. I’d much rather have you guys there than be alone.”

“Okay, then. It’s almost a two-hour ride out there. Want us to pick you up? Say around eight?”

“Sounds perfect. I’ll pack us some lunches.”

“Great,” Maddox said. With that, Wilder groaned and put more of his weight onto Maddox. “Okay, big guy, how about you not fall asleep right now?”

“Sleep good. You bothering me bad.”

“You’re such an asshole. Come on, hold it together for the five minutes it’ll take me to get you to the truck.”

Wilder groaned again but stood on his own. “See you tomorrow, Jazzy Scooter.” Then he walked away from them and toward the exit.

“Jazzy Scooter?” Jaz asked Maddox.

“You better hope he forgets that nickname by morning.” Both of them laughed. “We’ll see you tomorrow. Call if anything changes.”

“Will do. Good luck with him.”

Maddox quickly said goodbyes to everyone else as he tried to catch up with Wilder, who was probably passed out in the truck by now. Once he got outside, he saw Wild leaning against the passenger door. "Forget you have keys too?"

"I left them in the glove box. Such a bad decision."

"You have to move so I can open your door," Maddox said as he hit the unlock button on his truck's key fob.

Wild didn't step forward but rather slid toward the back of the truck so he wasn't blocking the door. Once Mad opened it, Wild practically fell inside and curled up as best he could on the seat.

Maddox shook his head at his friend before closing the door and walking around to the driver's side and climbing in. As he steered them toward home, Maddox found himself anticipating hiking with Jaz the next day. She had a sincerity to her Maddox couldn't deny being drawn to. It didn't hurt that she clearly liked to hike, which was one of Mad's favorite downtime activities.

Add in the fact that he got to include the joker next to him, and it had the trappings of being a perfect way to spend his day. Maddox glanced over at Wilder, who had his eyes closed tight, his breathing even and steady as they drove down the street toward home. The guy was a fucking handful, but Maddox wouldn't change a single thing about him.

"Mad?" Wilder asked, even though Maddox had been sure he'd been sleeping.

"Yeah?"

"Don't let me forget about calling her Jazzy Scooter, okay? That nickname is gold."

A laugh rumbled through Mad's chest. "I won't, buddy."

CHAPTER EIGHT

"Morning," Jasmine said as she pulled open the door to Maddox's truck and hopped up into the seat.

"Shh," came a soft voice from the passenger's seat.

"Good morning," Mad said. "Don't mind him." He nodded toward Wild, who was leaning against the door with sunglasses on and a hat pulled down lower than would be considered normal. "He's grumpy."

"I'm hungover."

Jaz laughed. "I thought you guys said Wilder doesn't get hangovers?"

"There's a first time for everything," Wild said.

"Just face it," Mad said. "You're getting old. Your body fights back now when you beat up on it." Maddox pulled down the street, and Jaz saw him glimpse at her in the mirror. Though she couldn't see his mouth, the crinkle to his eyes told her he was grinning. He was baiting Wild, and even Jaz knew Wild would bite.

"I'm not *old*. I'm only twenty-eight. You're five years older than me."

"That just means both of us are old."

Wild let out an annoyed groan before tilting his head in Jaz's direction and asking, "What do you think?"

She thought for a moment before replying, "I think you're both old now."

"You're fired," Wild joked before pulling his cap down even lower and announcing that there needed to be more sleeping and less talking for the remainder of the drive.

The truck was quiet for a while with Maddox driving, Wild snoring softly, and Jaz listening to music on her phone. When she saw Maddox look back at her, she could tell he'd said something. She pulled her headphones out so she could hear him. "I'm sorry?"

"I just asked what you packed for lunch."

"Oh, um, homemade chicken salad sandwiches, some peanut butter and jelly, and some fruit and stuff. I didn't know what you guys would want, and I didn't think to ask last night." She leaned forward, craning her neck to see if Wilder was still sleeping. "Shouldn't we be quiet? He looks like he's still asleep."

"He's not," Maddox said confidently. "He'd still be snoring if he was."

"Really?"

"I *don't* snore," came a groggy voice.

Mad and Jasmine were silent for a moment before they both burst out laughing.

"I thought I fired you," Wild said, turning around to look at Jasmine, who was just now calming down. "Don't you feel awkward going hiking with your previous employer?"

Jaz smiled. "Not really."

"I rehired her while you were napping," Mad said.

"I hate you both."

Maddox put a hand on Wilder's shoulder and squeezed, pushing his body back and forth. "Don't say things you don't mean."

"I may throw up if you keep doing that."

Stopping immediately, Maddox said, "Now that's something I believe."

For the rest of the drive, they discussed the new classes at the gym that would begin this week, as well as the online registration site Jaz had managed to get up and running. Since she hadn't started teaching classes yet, she had time during the day to find a program that would allow clients to register easily. Then they played the car game—an appropriately named competition, Wilder explained, that involved each person choosing a color and counting the number of vehicles they saw with that color. Maddox was currently in the lead with eight white vehicles, and Wild was in second with six black. Jasmine still had none.

"Who picks yellow?" Wild asked when they pulled into a parking space at Canyon Falls a half hour later, officially putting an end to their game.

Jasmine shrugged. "I like yellow."

She grabbed her backpack out of the back seat and put it over her shoulders. The men did the same, and before long, they were heading toward the trail the guys had recommended.

"You seem like you feel better," Jaz said to Wilder.

"Yeah, not too bad. I slept a lot of it off. Just a little headache now, but it'll pass."

Jasmine pulled her backpack off one shoulder and reached into the front pocket. Without explanation, she handed him the glass vial, knowing he'd most likely question what the hell it was. "This should help."

Wild looked at the small blue bottle she'd given him. "Uh, Jaz, we have a zero-tolerance drug policy at Transform...sooo I'm gonna have to let you go. Again."

"It's not drugs," she said with an eye roll. "It's an oil for your headache. Just roll it over your forehead and your jaw if you feel tension there."

"What's in it?" he asked, removing the cap and bringing it to his nose. "Doesn't *smell* like cocaine."

"It doesn't look like it either, you moron," Maddox said. "That stuff really work?" he asked her. "Or is it just like a mind over body thing? I have a buddy whose wife is pretty into all that, but I don't know much about it."

"Yeah, it really does work. There's medical research to back it up and everything. I told you how I use it in yoga classes, but it's a part of my life. I teach classes on them now. I'd be happy to show you how it all works sometime if you're interested in natural alternatives to medicine and cleaning products and stuff. There's a huge health benefit to them, and you could actually work them into the gym as a way to help people reach fitness goals or lose weight or detox. The possibilities are really endless." Jaz had to stop herself from talking because she realized she was rambling, and once she started on a subject she was passionate about, it was difficult for her to keep quiet.

"That'd be great," Mad said. "I might have to take you up on that."

"Awesome, yeah, we'll sit down one day, and I'll show you

everything." She glanced over at Wilder, who still seemed to be deciding whether to put it on his skin. "It's just peppermint," she assured him. "I save the cyanide for people I don't like."

Wild nodded cautiously but rolled the oil on his head before giving it back to her so they could continue walking. "Thanks," he said. "Guess it can't hurt."

Once again, she found herself in between the men, and she realized how comfortable she felt there—both of them by her side to talk to and to protect her if a bear or reclusive lunatic jumped out and tried to attack her. They continued on the trail for the next twenty minutes or so, climbing higher up the small mountain, which was thick with greenery.

Finally, the trail narrowed so much they had to walk in a line, rather than side by side. Maddox took the front, with Wilder following behind him. For a moment, it felt strange to be trailing them rather than arm to arm like they'd been last night at the bar and for much of their walk so far. But she couldn't have been happier when she noticed the view. And she wasn't thinking about the beautiful trees or the way the rays of sun peeked through the leaves as it brightened the morning sky.

Nope. She was talking about the perfect view of Mad's and Wild's asses. Even with their backpacks on, she could gaze at them—*study* them, even—without the guys noticing. She'd obviously caught glimpses of them when they'd been at the gym, but it wasn't like staring at her bosses' butts was an acceptable workplace behavior.

"How ya doin' back there, Scooter?"

It took Jasmine a few seconds—and Wild turning around

to face her—before she realized he was talking to her, but she immediately started laughing. Her reaction was more due to the nickname he'd unfortunately remembered than to her appraisal of him and Maddox, which she was sure he knew nothing about.

"You remembered on your own." Maddox laughed, sounding impressed. He kept walking, forcing the other two to keep going so they didn't fall behind.

"Yup, and it's a good thing I did. You weren't any help."

"I kinda figured Jaz wasn't that fond of the name, so I was gonna let her off the hook."

"No way," Wilder said. "Scooter's a great name. It's cute." He turned around to face her again, walking backward as he gave her one of his signature grins that showed off his dimples. "Fits you perfectly. Now come on," he said excitedly. "We're almost to the top. You'll love it."

Jasmine couldn't disagree. She already loved it.

For the next ten minutes or so, Maddox led them up the trail, stopping a few times to point out some poison oak and sumac, which Jasmine said she wasn't familiar with. He liked teaching her a few things, and she seemed appreciative of the lesson. Wild, on the other hand, added to the moment by stating that he'd gotten poison ivy on his balls once and Jasmine would be smart to pay attention so the same thing didn't happen to her.

"She doesn't have balls," Maddox said.

"Well, yeah. But she has...other parts that probably won't feel good with poison anything on them either."

“Thanks, Doctor,” Mad said, making Jaz laugh.

“I do appreciate you guys going with me, though. I don’t have the best sense of direction, so I probably would’ve wandered around until I found my car again. And I might’ve been covered in poison oak when I got back.”

Maddox chuckled, but he couldn’t help thinking about Jasmine getting lost out here, her beautiful skin marred by something she could’ve avoided. Not to mention the fact that there were some animals out here that wouldn’t be fun to run into, especially by herself. It made his eyes wander to the brush surrounding them as they walked the rest of the quarter mile to the top. He stopped and pointed when he saw what he was looking for. He didn’t think he’d ever made it the whole trail without seeing one. “Snake,” he said.

At some point during their journey, Jaz had found her way behind him again, probably when he was teaching her about the various plants. But now she was right on him, practically trying to climb him. If she could’ve found a way to get higher, Mad was certain she would have. He tried not to laugh at her fear, reminding himself that not everyone had experience in the wilderness. He also tried not to think about how good it felt to have her body pressed against his. But that was a futile effort. He was conscious of how close her mouth was to his ear. If she hadn’t been screaming in it, he would’ve been turned on. “It’s okay. There’s nothing to be afraid of.”

When Jasmine started ranting about how she hated snakes and they were disgusting creatures that were venomous, Maddox said, “I was talking to the snake. I think your squealing scared him.”

Jaz tried to release her hold on him for long enough to smack him, but it only resulted in her pushing her fist into him until she gave up and opened her hand so she could take hold of him again.

"It's really okay," he said, serious this time. "I don't even know where it went."

"That's more frightening than being able to see it."

"What you don't know can't hurt you," Wild said.

"That's completely untrue," Jaz yelled behind her. "You two just gave me a whole lesson on poisonous plants. And I saw an article not that long ago that snakes have been hiding in people's pool noodles if they leave them out."

"She's got a point." Maddox walked a minute or so with Jaz on his back before she finally slid slowly down his back to the ground. It was probably the most action Maddox had gotten in a few months, and his body responded as such, immediately missing Jasmine's body on his and her breath against his skin.

Jaz was in awe when they finally got to the top of the trail. She stood near the edge of the canyon, taking in the view, which was probably several miles on a day as clear as this one. The small waterfall cascaded down to the bottom, where it pooled in crystal-clear water. The peacefulness seemed to permeate every cell of Maddox's body as the three stood silently in the sun, a sheen of sweat on each of them from the humidity and the exertion of their hike. A soft breeze blew at their backs, and Maddox tried to remember the last time he'd felt this content.

But the moment didn't last long because Wild interrupted it with, "I think I have a tick in my ass."

Maddox and Jaz turned to where Wilder stood to their

left, a hand down the back of his pants.

"Seriously?" Mad asked. "Like *in* your ass or *on* it?"

"On it, but *in* it, if that makes sense. I wouldn't lie about something as serious as that."

"It's not serious. It's a tick. You'll be fine."

"I need one of you to cut it out," Wild said, an urgency to his voice that wasn't there a few seconds ago. "It's already engorged with the blood of my butt."

"That's disgusting," Mad said. "And I'm not going anywhere near your hairy ass. You'll have to go to the doctor or something when we get back. I draw the line at picking bugs out of your private areas." He was just teasing Wild because he knew it would get a rise out of him, and he seemed to be losing more and more of his composure as the seconds passed.

Wilder opened his mouth to protest, but Jasmine cut him off before he could. "I'll do it."

"No," both Wild and Mad said in unison, though probably for very different reasons. "You won't recover from this," Mad added.

"Hey," Wilder said. "My ass isn't some hairy thing she won't recover from." He looked to Jaz, his expression pleading with her to help him.

Maddox shook his head at his friend. For a big guy, Wilder could definitely be a baby sometimes. He thought about how Wild never would've lasted in the military, but that fact wasn't a recent revelation. On many occasions, Wilder had admitted that himself. The routine, the strict authority... Nothing about the military was in Wild's wheelhouse. Maddox, on the other hand, had loved the training and brotherhood that couldn't be replicated anywhere else. He'd thrived on it. That was, until he hadn't. As much as the army had added to his life—made him become a better man—he'd lost pieces of himself to it too. He had seen things—had endured things—that he couldn't forget no matter how much he wanted to. And those things had not only messed with *him*, they'd also fucked up one of the most important relationships he'd ever had.

He'd never be able to forgive himself for what happened as a result of his inability to be the man he should've been when he'd returned to the States. It was why he'd vowed to himself that he'd never get involved with a woman again beyond something strictly physical. He was way too fucked up to contribute positively to a relationship. And up until now, he hadn't wanted to. His interest in women had been limited mostly to physical attraction, and he'd never kept that a secret from anyone he slept with. He was always up front about his intentions.

But something felt different with Jasmine. Not only was she attractive—incredibly so—she checked all of Maddox's boxes. That was, if he had boxes he was looking to check. She knew how to work hard, but she knew how to have fun too. She was independent and motivated, and there was a light to her that allowed her to see the glass half-full, while Mad sometimes couldn't even see a glass at all. He almost laughed out loud at the realization that Jaz was like the female version of Wild. Which, as scary as that was, explained why Maddox found himself drawn to her.

Well, that and the fact that having her here meant it wasn't Maddox who had to have his face near Wilder's ass. Maddox felt so horrible for her. "I'll do it," Mad said, like it was more of a burden than it actually was. He'd seen much worse in the army than a tick in someone's ass.

He pulled out his Swiss Army Knife and began to open it, when Wild yelled, "Wait, wait, wait! Let's see what her way is first." He looked at Jaz, his eyes pleading with her to go easy on him. "Does your way involve digging sharp objects into my skin?"

"Nope," Jaz replied, already looking through her backpack. Instead of removing something sharp to dig out the tick, she had a small bottle in her hand. She must've recognized Wild's confusion, because she held up the bottle and said, "Peppermint oil."

"Again? Does my butt smell that bad?" Wilder asked, his pants low enough for Jaz to get to the tick.

Maddox and Jasmine burst out laughing, and Jaz said, "No. Your butt is fine. Peppermint makes ticks crawl right out of your skin."

"Really? Cures headaches and removes ticks? That's crazy." Mad was intrigued, and against his better judgment, he moved closer to Wild's bare ass. "I'm actually surprised it didn't just crawl right out when it realized it was biting into your ass."

Wild ignored the comment and instead asked, "You're filming this, right?"

"No, I'm not filming it," Maddox said. "There's no way I'm gonna have a video of you with your pants down on my phone."

"But I need to see this, and I can't because of the angle. Please," he begged like a child asking for candy at the checkout line of a store. "You can delete it as soon as you send it to me. You're gonna watch it anyway. What's the difference if you film it too?"

"Fine," Maddox groaned, taking his phone out like the video was more of a hardship than it actually was. It wasn't the first time he'd seen Wilder without clothes on, and unfortunately it probably wouldn't be the last. When they'd first moved in together, Wild went weeks before he finally listened to Maddox when he insisted he stay clothed around him. The man slept naked and often didn't feel the need to dress before making his way to the bathroom or to get a cup of coffee in the morning, insisting that if he didn't care, why should Maddox.

"Oh shit," Maddox said a few seconds after Jaz put a few drops of oil on Wild's cheek. "That's nuts. It's moving around. It looks like this might work."

A few seconds later, the little guy detached from Wild's skin, and Jasmine grabbed it with a tissue. "All done," she said, wiping away the excess oil. "You were a great patient."

Wild pulled up his pants and buckled his belt before turning back around to face them. Seconds later, he was begging to see the video, his body already positioned between Mad and Jaz with his arms around their shoulders. "That's fucking sweet," he said after watching the tick detach itself from his flesh. "Your camera skills are on point." Then he squeezed both their shoulders and said, "This was like one of those community-building adventures in nature. Don't you feel so much closer after this?"

"So close," Mad said dryly, causing Jasmine to burst out

laughing and Wild to roll his eyes at Mad's sarcasm.

"This guy thinks he's so funny," Wild said to Jaz, a thumb pointed in Maddox's direction.

"I think he's funny too," Jasmine said.

Her compliment—and smile that accompanied it—did things to Maddox that he wished he could ignore.

CHAPTER NINE

"What's on these chips?" Jaz asked Mad and Wild as she slowly chewed a tortilla chip the waitress had brought out.

"The more important questions is, why are you eating them?" Wild, the nutrition drill sergeant, asked.

Jaz rolled her eyes. She was all for treating the body like a temple, and such treatment had definitely paid off in Wild's case, but he was a little over the top about it sometimes. With the exception of how he took his coffee, of course.

Maddox grabbed a chip and took a bite. "Lime."

"Thank you," Jaz said, over-enunciating the words. She popped the rest of the chip into her mouth. "I don't like it," she added before reaching for another one.

"Then why are you having more?" Wild asked.

"Because it bothers you." She stuffed the chip into her mouth and smiled widely at him.

Maddox's raspy laugh sounded beside her. She loved making that man laugh. He didn't do nearly enough of it, in her opinion. "Going to a restaurant with you two is like eating with toddlers," he said as he dipped a chip in salsa.

"Those chips are probably covered in salt. Good luck finding your abs tomorrow."

Mad smiled at him. "I never have trouble finding my abs."

"Such a cocky bastard," Wild grumbled.

Maddox shrugged before loading more salsa onto another chip.

Jaz watched the two of them for a moment, immensely happy that life had brought her to this town and to these men. Ever since their hike, they'd spent most of their free time together. Granted, all of them having free time at the *same* time was a bit of an anomaly, but they managed. Jaz was starting to get a sneaking suspicion that Mad was intentionally scheduling them to have similar time off, but she didn't feel inclined to ask. Maddox came off as a little skittish about certain things—like being sweet enough to make time to hang out with her—and she didn't want to call attention to it only to have him stop doing it so he didn't seem like a sap.

Considering how out of place Jaz had felt most of her life, the fact that she seemed to fit in perfectly with these two complicated men surprised the hell out of her. And they were definitely complicated. Maddox sometimes went dark and brooding out of nowhere, and Wild sometimes got agitated when he was too still, which could be exhausting to keep up with. But Jaz found these things almost endearing—like jagged pieces of a larger puzzle that Jaz knew was worth putting together.

"What can I get you guys?" the server asked, startling Jaz from her thoughts.

"Can I have the steak tacos, please?" Jaz requested.

"Rice and beans okay?" the server asked.

"Perfect." Jaz handed the young woman her menu.

"And what about for you, handsome?"

Jaz's head jerked up to look at the woman, who was smiling seductively at Wild. Jaz felt her eyes narrowing. This chick looking at Wild that way was rubbing Jaz all wrong. A possessiveness bubbled up within her, and despite Jaz telling herself she had no rights to such feelings—had no claim to Wild—it didn't dampen the sensation at all. Jaz wanted to rip this girl's arms off and beat her to death with them.

Taking a calming breath, Jaz brought her gaze down to Wild. She watched a smirk start to curve his lips, but then his eyes met hers, and his lips drew flat. "I'll have the chicken tacos. Hold the rice and beans." He handed the menu back to the server without taking his eyes off Jaz. It seemed like they were engaged in a smoldering game of chicken until Wild crossed his eyes and gave her a dopey look.

The spell between them broke as Jaz chuckled quietly. She looked over at Maddox, who ordered a bean burrito. Maddox winked at her as he handed the server his menu without turning toward her.

Jaz felt her cheeks blush. It was overwhelming to have the attention of these two men, even if that attention was playful and sweet instead of something more intense, like she wanted.

The realization had been a little jarring for her, the moment she'd accepted she was drawn to both of these men who offered her very different things. She'd been lying in bed, staring at the ceiling and thinking over the day they'd spent playing Ultimate Frisbee in a nearby park, and it had hit her with astounding clarity: she was attracted to Maddox *and* Wilder.

And while the attraction seemed like a fluid thing—

sometimes drawing her more to Mad one second and Wild the next—at the end of the day the playing field leveled out. She honestly didn't prefer the company of one over the other. She liked them like this: all hanging out and spending time together. And it made her supremely happy that they seemed to enjoy the same thing.

♦♦♦♦

Maddox leaned back in his chair, dropping his napkin on his empty plate, and watched Jaz and Wild argue about whether or not they were having dessert.

"We gotta," Jaz said. "They have an apple burrito."

"Who cares?" Wild asked. "That's basically like an apple pie. You can get that anytime."

"Yes. Like now."

"You can't still be hungry. You're like a hundred and twenty pounds."

"Hundred and twenty-five. Twenty-six after I have my burrito."

"Your job is to promote good nutrition in clients. You need to lead by example."

Maddox smiled. He could tell Wild was more enjoying giving her a hard time than actually criticizing her wanting the dessert.

Jaz sighed heavily. "It's not *that* unhealthy. It has fruit in it, for Christ's sake."

"Fruit that is surrounded by fried dough that's been coated in cinnamon and topped with ice cream."

"Sounds delicious."

Wild snorted. "Deliciously artery-clogging."

Jaz picked up a fork and pointed the tines at Wilder. "Let's get something straight, Wilder Vaughn. I'm here for a good time, not a long time."

Wild threw his hands up and looked over at Maddox. "There's no reasoning with her."

Jaz started dancing in her seat. "That means I win." She waved the server over and ordered her burrito. When it arrived, she stared down at it like it was a pot of gold. "Apple burrito. You get in my belly."

"And then stay there like a brick," Wild murmured.

"Don't let the mean man try to make you feel bad," she said to the dessert. "You make yourself at home in there." Jaz took a big bite and moaned as the dessert slid down her throat.

The sound made Maddox's dick twitch, and he desperately hoped she didn't make that sound after every bite. Having a hard-on at the dinner table wasn't exactly high on his to-do list.

"Come on, guys. You know you want some." Jaz taunted them with her fork full of apples and dough.

Wilder tracked the movement of her hand. "We don't want your empty calories."

"Yes, you do," she sang. She moved the fork in front of him again, and this time Wilder snagged her wrist and wrapped his lips around the dessert. Jaz stared at him wide-eyed. "Oh my God. I broke you. Are you okay? Do we need to find you a twelve-step program or something?"

"Shut up," Wild muttered before grabbing a fork of his own and filling it with a heap of apple burrito.

Maddox laughed at their antics. Hanging out with these

two was fun. He'd always enjoyed hanging out with Wilder, but Jaz fit in with them so seamlessly it was like she'd always been friends with them. If only he could do something about his pesky attraction to her, everything would be perfect.

Mad couldn't deny that the more time he spent with Jaz, the more he felt drawn to her. It was a little alarming for him. He hadn't felt like that about anyone since he'd been discharged from the army, and he thought he likely never would. After his life had gone sideways and he'd struggled—with the help of Wild—to get himself straightened out again, he'd felt sexually attracted to women, but that was where it ended. It was like the intimate, romantic part of him had broken when the rest of him had. But now that part was beginning to heal, and while he was thrilled at the possibility of having these feelings for someone else, he also didn't want to ruin what the three of them had together.

The sound of a fork clattering on the table in front of him jolted him out of his thoughts. He darted his gaze up to Wild's.

"If you think you're getting out of here without eating some of this, you're crazy," Wild said to him, a sparkle of mischief alight in his eyes.

Mad smirked and picked up the fork, helping himself to a giant bite of the burrito.

"Hey!" Jaz yelled. "Don't you two dare eat all my burrito."

Wild responded by piling a giant portion of apples and ice cream on his fork and slowly bringing it toward his mouth. Jaz reached across the table and smacked the fork out of his hand before it reached his lips.

They all stared wide-eyed at where the fork fell to the

floor. Then Mad and Wild turned to gawk at Jaz, who shrugged. "I panicked."

The three of them erupted in laughter, and Maddox became even more convinced that he shouldn't do anything to jeopardize their friendship. What they had would be more than enough for him.

CHAPTER TEN

"Thirty-one, thirty-two, thirty-three, thirty-four, thirty-five." Wild finished with the last punch to Maddox's arm, but even though he and Jaz had been alternating, she joined in for the last one.

"Hey, I'm only thirty-four." Maddox immediately began rubbing his arm where Wild had been hitting him before switching to massage the other arm where Jaz had been hitting him.

"It's good luck," Jaz explained at the same time that Wilder explained that since Mad had just begun his thirty-fifth year, he needed the punch to start of the next year of his life correctly.

Maddox looked skeptical when he said, "That seems like something you made up because you wanted to hit me as many times as possible."

Wild did his best to look offended. "Does that sound like something I'd do?"

"Yes," Mad replied.

"You're not giving Jazzy Scooter a hard time about punching you an extra time. It's because she's prettier than me, isn't it?" Like most things, Wild didn't think before he said the words. It had been an instinctual joke to make, but it felt borderline inappropriate because they were true. Not only was Jaz their employee, but Wild was also more and more attracted to her with each passing day. And it wasn't just physical either, which in all honesty, scared the ever-loving fuck out of him. Wild was a no-strings-attached kind of guy—always had been. More was complicated, and who the hell needed complicated? But his feelings for Jaz were becoming all kinds of complicated, and he hoped like hell he wasn't as obvious about it as he felt.

Jaz rolled her eyes and said, "I'm not answering to that stupid nickname." Turning to Mad, she continued, "You ready to go, birthday boy?"

Wild was thankful for the change in subject. It wasn't that he couldn't admit to himself that he was conflicted, but tonight wasn't about him and his relationship-phobias. It was about showing Mad that he had people in his corner. With no living family he knew of, Mad would likely just as soon let his birthday pass uncelebrated, but Wild wasn't having it. And this year when Wild suggested they invite Jaz along so they could give her a taste of the city's nightlife, Mad had readily agreed.

Wild was excited to spend the time with her too because they always had a great time together. But now that she was standing next to him in an incredibly short black dress that revealed almost her entire back and shoulders, it was more than his mind that was becoming excited.

He'd seen Jasmine in tight clothing almost daily since she'd started at Transform. And he'd seen her in clothing that wasn't gym attire plenty of times by this point, but this outfit might have been one of the sexiest he'd seen on a woman. The bottom molded to her like it had been made especially for her body—tight against the curves of her hips and her perfectly round ass. The top was looser with thin straps that draped the shiny fabric over the front of her body and sides. He tried not to think too much about whether she was wearing a bra, because the only conclusion he could come to was "not a fucking chance," and he didn't trust himself not to let his gaze drop to her breasts. Wild knew that beneath those clothes was a body that allowed every move she made to be fluid and graceful, like her every step was a practiced dance that few people were capable of performing. It made him wonder how she moved in other circumstances...on the dance floor...in bed.

He needed to get a handle on himself.

Shaking himself, he checked his Uber app and saw that it was right around the corner. When it pulled up, Wild motioned for Jaz to get in ahead of him. He wasn't a good enough liar to tell himself he was just being a gentleman. The thought of seeing Jasmine from behind again—her long dark hair cascading down her smooth, tan back had his cock begging for some attention. Fuck, it was gonna be a long night.

♦♦♦♦

Avenue 22 was about fifteen minutes away from Mad and Wild's apartment, but they didn't go there as often as they used to. A few years ago, it had been one of their favorite places to spend a Saturday night. But once they'd opened their own gym, their aging bodies couldn't recover from a night out like they used to, even if Maddox didn't ever drink that much. The lack of control that accompanied alcohol hadn't ever held much of an appeal to him, especially after he'd come home. Plus, the late nights—and the women who'd ended up in their beds—just didn't mesh with five a.m. personal training sessions. And they owed it to their clients to give them their all. It made this night even more special because it had been at least six months since they'd been here. Mad could let himself loosen up a bit tonight without letting go completely. He knew where his line was.

Jasmine was the first to the bar, grabbing three of something that looked too colorful for Maddox to possibly enjoy. He was more of a beer guy, or maybe the occasional shot of whiskey. But whatever Jaz was handing him certainly wasn't either. "First round's on me," she said, setting the glasses down on the low table Wild had reserved for them in advance. "I'd like to give a toast."

"Don't do this," Mad begged, a hand over his forehead in embarrassment. "My birthday doesn't require a toast."

"Shut up." She smiled, giving him a slap to the thigh. "It's your birthday, and I'll toast if I want to."

Wilder's eyebrows narrowed. "I think you have the lyrics wrong."

"You shut up too," she warned with a point of her finger. "Maddox," she began. "I couldn't think of a better way to begin my new life in a new city. You're a fantastic boss and an even better guy."

"This speech is sickening," Wild complained.

But luckily, Jaz continued, her eyes glistening in the lights as she looked at Mad. "Thanks for making me feel so welcome at Transform. But more than that, thanks for being a friend in a place where I didn't have any."

He noticed the way whatever she had on her lips

shimmered as she spoke. Plump, pink, and wet. Maddox wanted to blame the alcohol for his fantasies about what it would be like to have them around his cock, but he knew the few drinks he'd had couldn't be to blame.

"You deserve the best birthday," she said, raising her glass. "To Maddox."

"To Maddox," Wild repeated, raising his drink to his best friend.

"Thanks, guys. I'm glad to have you both here."

Maddox finished whatever sweet, fruity mix Jasmine had gotten for him and then downed the beer Wilder had bought him after insisting Mad wouldn't pay for a thing tonight. They talked as best they could over the loud music, but much of the time, Maddox just enjoyed being in the company of his best friend and the beautiful woman he was coming to know more about each day. Jasmine was still milking the drink she'd gotten herself when they'd first arrived, bringing the straw to her mouth and sucking slowly.

Shifting in his seat, he tried to adjust himself to a position that didn't have his cock pressing against his pants in a way that made him want to rub himself until he got some relief. But his fitted jeans didn't seem to cooperate, and he wondered how he was ever going to make it the rest of the night like this. "Who wants to dance?" Maddox asked, needing to move, though he knew that it probably wasn't the best idea right now, especially if Jasmine took him up on it.

"I'll go," Jaz said, and Wild told them he'd be out when his beer was done.

Maddox didn't expect Jasmine to grab his hand on their

way out to the dance floor, to entwine her fingers with his as they walked. But the feel of her skin on his had his heart beating so rapidly he swore he could feel the blood flowing through his veins. As they weaved through the crowd, Mad's anticipation grew.

Jasmine moved slowly at first, despite the music's fast tempo. It was a seductive dance that she seemed to be doing more for herself than for anyone around her. Her eyes closed, and her body seemed to unwind with the passing seconds. She looked lost in every delicate movement, her hands running over her own body, down her torso and over the top of her thighs. His mind told Mad to look anywhere else but directly at her, but every cell in his body screamed otherwise. They danced close to one another, but they hadn't touched yet, and it was driving Maddox crazy. He knew it was only a matter of time before his hands navigated to her hips, pulling her in closer until their bodies touched.

Another song passed, and he could feel the heat between them. It wasn't only from the dancing. There was a pull he could feel with every pulse of the music. It drove him closer to her, made him give in to the temptation he'd tried so hard to resist. And now his hand was on her hip, his fingers stroking over her exposed lower back. A few inches lower, and his fingers would've found a much more intimate area.

His touch was gentle at first as he gauged her response. And when she moved closer to him instead of pulling away, his entire body was ablaze with desire. He could feel the bit of sweat on her skin, and the thought of tasting her—running his tongue over her salty flesh—had him on fire. Her breasts pressed against his chest, and he was certain she could feel his erection, because fuck if she wasn't swaying back and forth over it.

Every brush over him had Mad wanting to pull her against him and keep her there until he exploded. The fact that he didn't give a shit that they were in full view of others indicated to him that Jasmine had an effect on him that few women did. He was wound so fucking tight, so high from the alcohol and the feel of Jaz's body against his. It wasn't long before he was kissing her, their tongues exploring each other in a way that felt like Mad was both consuming her and *being* consumed. It was an odd paradox—and one that had him wanting more than either of them would ever do on a dance floor.

But for now, he was content to enjoy the way her mouth joined his, the way her hands roamed over his chest and down to the hem of his shirt. His mind was begging her to lift it up, run her fingertips on the ridges of his abs, and scratch her nails over his shoulder blades and the muscles of his back.

He groaned into her mouth when her hands reached down to the sides of his thighs before making their way up to the back of his neck to feel the short hair at the bottom of his head. The touch and the vibration of the music had him buzzing inside and out. Beating against his chest, his heart was going way too fast for the speed they were moving.

Maddox tried to control his dick, but it was impossible. It strained against his jeans, begging for attention he was sure he'd have to give it later. When their kiss finally broke, their lips stayed so close to the other's that Maddox could still taste the strawberry and mint on her breath from her drink.

He wanted to ask her what the hell had just happened, but his body wouldn't let him. It was warring with the logical side of his brain that told him this shouldn't be happening. So he let his body speak for him: his teeth nipped at her bottom lip, and he ran his tongue over her jaw, causing her head to tilt back for him. And his cock...well, there was no fucking way his cock would let him stop what was happening between them.

Even if Wilder had just come out to dance with them.

Jasmine was so hot, so wet with her desire for Maddox, that she hadn't noticed Wilder come up behind her until Maddox gave a nod over Jasmine's shoulder. She looked behind her but didn't break contact with Mad. Her body liked his way too much to pull away. So instead, she reached back to grab Wild's hand, pulling him in toward her so he could join them.

He seemed hesitant at first, probably feeling as though he was intruding on an intimate moment. If only he knew how wrong he was—how his presence there only made the moment *more* intimate. She wanted both of them—had always wanted both—and the night felt more complete when she found herself between them again.

The dance was cautious at first as the men seemed unclear of their place in it. But to her, it all seemed so natural, so she showed them what she wanted. She moved Wilder's hand to her stomach, entwining her fingers with his and then placing her hand over his before letting go completely. From there, Wild found his own rhythm, pressing her against him as he danced. Wild was just as aroused as Maddox, and the thought made her close her eyes to tune out everything except what she felt: the pounding of the bass, the fuzziness in her mind, the hard cocks grinding against her.

Soon, hands and lips were everywhere. She'd leaned back to give Wilder access to her neck, and he'd taken her invitation, his hand lightly holding her throat as he kissed along her jawline to her lips. Maddox had her hand, kissing up her forearm to her collarbone and chest. She'd told Wilder not that long ago that she wanted to find enlightenment, and this right here might be the closest she'd ever come. This right here was perfection.

♦♦♦♦

Wild's mind was blank. He was all feeling, all need. At least for a little while. Fuck if his best friend was there to watch. His dick certainly didn't care, so why should he? They were friends having fun, and Wilder was always up for fun. Especially when that fun involved a gorgeous woman's ass grinding against his hard cock. He wasn't sure if it was weird that Maddox was probably hard too and only inches from him. And he wasn't sure if it was weird that he was thinking of Maddox's dick while he was so fucking turned on, but since it didn't seem to have a negative effect on his own erection, he chose not to worry about it.

That was easy to do with the moans coming from Jasmine's lips. She seemed lost in the music, in the moment, and in what both he and Maddox were doing to her. Wild roamed his hands over every inch of Jaz's body he had access to, and he wondered what might have happened if they'd had more privacy. Would clothes have been discarded? Would any of them have come? Because Christ, that solo session he'd had in the shower had nothing on what he felt now.

His cock felt so fucking full, so ready as it ground between Jaz's ass cheeks. The scent of her shampoo, clean and fruity, was intoxicating, and he imagined what it would be like to bury his face in her hair while he thrust inside her until he came. Flashes of the club lights became flashes of Jasmine's face below his as he drove into her harder and harder until he was so deep he wondered if he could ever find his way out. Not that he'd want to. This was the sexiest fucking thing he'd done in a while. So he tried not to think about the fact that he was currently sharing a girl with his best friend or that he was a bedroom away from participating in his first threesome that wouldn't include two females.

The only thing that mattered was that he was enjoying himself. His hedonistic side screamed at him to keep going, while the more logical—though significantly less vocal—side nudged him kindly. *Think about what you're doing,* it whispered. *This could be bad for you. This could be bad for* all *of you.*

But Wild did what he'd done most of his life: told that pesky little voice to shut the fuck up and let him enjoy himself. If there was anything to worry about, he'd worry about it later.

And if *he* didn't worry about it, he knew his best friend would do enough worrying for both of them.

CHAPTER ELEVEN

Maddox was hot all over, his naked skin glistening with a sheen of sweat. His cock was hard, and his body was quivering with need. He screwed his eyes shut, trying to hold on to this feeling—this euphoric strain that preceded an epic release. Someone was blowing on his sensitive skin, causing goose bumps to dot his overheated body.

The gentle puffs of air were lower each time, teasing his nipples, ghosting over his abs, before blowing down his happy trail toward his aching shaft. The cooler air felt good on him, especially when it blew over his cock before a tongue darted out to lick at the head. That tongue was soon replaced by a warm mouth, which caused Maddox to bow off the bed. He felt the person's lips stretch around him, taking half of his thick cock before lifting off with an obscene pop.

Mad reached down and buried his fingers in hair he knew would be long before he even gripped it. He also knew it was dark without opening his eyes. Because the flutter in his chest beat out a rhythm that seemed to repeat a name over and over.

Jaz. Jaz. Jaz.

Unable to resist the urge to watch her bobbing up and down on his cock, Mad opened his eyes and took in the sight. He let his eyes lock with hers as she sucked and licked him like he was her favorite flavor lollipop. He was enraptured by her, loving the sight of her between his legs. It was making him impossibly harder as he inched closer to his orgasm.

Movement registered in his peripheral vision, and Mad lazily let his eyes drift to the corner of the room where someone else sat, fully clothed but avidly watching the show Jaz was putting on.

Wild.

Wild, who rubbed the palm of his hand over the bulge in his jeans and licked his lips. Wild, who was watching Jaz suck Mad's cock and was clearly getting off on it.

Maddox's shaft pulsed under the attention—as if it liked being part of this erotic display. Liked that someone else was witnessing Jaz worship Mad's cock. Gripping Jaz's hair tighter, Mad let his hips buck off the bed a bit, let himself fuck her mouth without giving her more than she could handle.

"Give it to me, Mad," Jaz whispered.

Mad thought he heard a "Fuck yeah" from the corner, but it was difficult to tell as blood thundered through his ears as his entire system prepared for him to flood her mouth with his come. Just one more second and he'd be there, ready to fall over the edge, ready for the release that felt like a long time coming, ready...

Maddox groaned as awareness seeped into him. He kept his eyes closed, trying to will himself back into his dream even though he knew it was no use. He was groggy, but the dream was already becoming a faded photograph, and his consciousness was hovering on the frayed edges.

Rolling to his back, he rubbed his hands over his face and

groaned. Had he really just had a sex dream about Jaz? *And Wild had been in it,* his pesky subconscious reminded him. For fuck's sake, what was wrong with him? His eyes opened into slits as he struggled to adjust to the light in the room. His tongue felt glued to the roof of his mouth, and his throat felt like he'd tried to gargle sandpaper. Forcing himself up, he sat on the edge of his bed for a moment, taking stock of his body. He didn't feel *too* horrible. He had a dull ache in his head, but that was pretty much it. A pretty tame punishment for letting himself get drunk last night.

Last night.

Images rolled into his mind like waves on a beach. Dancing with Jaz and Wild, kissing—watching Wild kiss Jaz, Mad kissing Jaz. More drinks, more dancing, more kissing. He'd enjoyed the fuck out of all of it, despite feeling like he shouldn't have. Logic told him the night had gotten completely out of control—had gone sideways even if it felt as if he was firmly right side up.

What in the actual fuck? He'd made out with his employee at the same time his best friend did. How could he not be horrified by that? It was completely unprofessional, not to mention weird as hell. He and Wild were close and had definitely shared details of their one-night stands, but they'd never shared a girl before, even if it was just kissing. And not just any girl, but Jaz—the girl Mad had real feelings for and was interested in beyond a good time.

Digging the heels of his palms into his eye sockets, Mad tried to calm himself down. Maybe he hadn't fucked everything up. They'd all been drunk, and things had gotten a little out of hand, but that didn't mean he'd ruined things with Jaz. Maybe they'd all be able to pretend that nothing happened and go on like things had been. Mad could continue getting to know Jaz until he found his balls and asked her out. Simple.

He stood and headed for his bathroom, where he brushed his teeth and took a shower. When he felt human again, he climbed out and dried off before pulling on a pair boxer briefs and basketball shorts.

Time to face the music.

With any luck, Wild would still be asleep and Mad could get a couple cups of coffee into himself before he had to pretend he wasn't turned inside out—both by what had happened the previous night and by his dream. But as he walked down the hall, he heard clanging coming from the kitchen and knew that luck wasn't going to be on his side.

"Morning," he murmured as he rounded the corner to the kitchen, his voice sounding raspy.

Wild whipped around as if Mad had startled him. "Oh, hey. Morning. The Keurig's already on."

"Thanks," Mad said as he grabbed his favorite mug and popped a K-cup in the machine.

"You want eggs?" Wild asked as he opened the fridge.

"Not hungry yet. I'll make something later."

Wild nodded as he set about his task, and silence fell between them.

It seemed as if they weren't going to talk about it, which suited Maddox just fine. Though he did wish they could find *something* to talk about. The air in the room was stifling with awkward tension.

Mad opened his mouth to ask about Wild's training schedule—anything to get on more normal ground—when a few bangs sounded from the living room. Someone was knocking on their door.

"Who the hell is that?" Wild asked as he headed in the direction of the door, Mad following close behind. Wilder pulled open the door to reveal Jaz with her hair pulled back in a ponytail, wearing a crop top and leggings.

"Hi," she said happily. "I figured you two would be wigging out this morning, so I brought doughnuts."

Wilder stepped back to let her in. "How would doughnuts keep us from wigging out? Not that we were."

Maddox nodded his agreement with Wild but kept his mouth shut since...well, since he'd been totally wigging out.

"It's impossible to be tense while eating doughnuts. It's been scientifically proven."

"By who?" Wild asked on a laugh. "And I'm not eating doughnuts. I'm making an omelet."

"So disciplined with your food," she said affectionately. "So wild every other way. You're a real study in contrasts. You both are."

"No contrasting here," Mad said. And it was the truth. Maddox was a control freak who'd let his guard down one goddamn night, and look at what had happened. Never again.

"Our little dirty dancing session last night would prove otherwise," Jaz said with a wide smile.

Mad groaned. "Can we not go there?"

"Oh, we're going there. Repeatedly, if I have my way." Jaz slid between them and waltzed into the kitchen like she owned the place, leaving Mad and Wild staring and gaping after her.

Finally, the two men panned back so they were looking at one another.

"Did she just say what I think she did?" Mad asked.

"God help us...yes."

♦♦♦♦

Those two dopes stood by their front door as if she was going to execute them if they followed her. She knew this was how they'd be this morning: both internally freaking out while externally remaining stoic.

But that attitude wasn't going to work for Jaz. Last night had been more than she ever could have hoped for. Had opened the door to a possibility she hadn't thought existed but was now flashing in her mind like a neon sign. ENTER HERE, it blinked at her. And she'd spent the entire night trying to figure out how she could drag these two men in with her. Finally, it occurred to her that she might have to do it by force. So she'd armed herself with doughnuts and a positive attitude and made her way over.

She set the doughnuts on the counter and grabbed paper towels—was there some bro-rule that said men weren't allowed to buy regular napkins? Then she propped her elbow on the counter and waited for them. It probably took them less than a minute to follow her, but it felt longer. When they entered the kitchen, she beamed a smile at them, grabbed herself a doughnut, and took a big bite out of it.

She could see Maddox's chest heave with his sigh, but he stepped toward her and scanned the treats. "Is that a powdered

Bavarian cream?"

"Why yes, it is." Jaz had been thrilled with herself that she'd remembered Maddox had nearly salivated when they'd stopped at a diner one day that had a selection of desserts—doughnuts included. He'd debated getting himself one for almost fifteen minutes before deciding he was full.

"You don't play fair," he muttered before picking up the doughnut and taking a huge bite, moaning as he tasted it. "This is amazing."

She smiled at him before turning her gaze to Wild and arching an eyebrow at him. "How about you, Wild Man? I got some with strawberry filling so you could pretend you were eating fruit."

Wild rolled his eyes at her but peered into the box. He chose a twisted glazed one. "When in Rome," he said.

Jaz stood up straight and clapped her hands together. "Great. Now that your mouths are otherwise occupied, I can say what I came here to say."

Both men groaned, but Jaz ignored them. She had more pressing things to accomplish than fixing their petulant tendencies.

"To begin, I want to put it out there that I had a really good time last night. I *always* have a good time when I'm with you guys. And I don't want to do anything to jeopardize that."

"Agreed," Wild said as he chewed. Mad nodded.

"Good. I'm glad we're on the same page. So I think the only logical thing for us to do is to all date and see where it goes."

Mad immediately began choking on his doughnut, and Wild's eyes grew large before he forced what was in his mouth down his throat. Wild smacked Mad on the back a few times to no avail.

"You should put your arms up," Jaz suggested.

"My arms?" Mad choked out. "What the...fuck my arms."

Oookay, so maybe she should've eased into this better.

Mad finally got himself under control and drank some water Wild had gotten him.

Then Wilder turned his attention to her. "Are you serious? You think we should...all... Are you crazy?"

Probably. "Why is all of us dating crazy? We've basically been doing just that for over a month."

"We have *not* been dating. We've just been hanging out... as friends," Wild argued.

"Is that really how you both view me? As just your friend?" Jaz looked at them both seriously. This was the make-or-break moment. Because while she knew she was insanely attracted to them, she wasn't positive they felt the same.

"Isn't that what you are?" Mad asked.

"Yeah, I guess. But is that all you *want* me to be?"

Mad held her gaze but didn't answer. He looked over at Wild, and the two men stared at one another as if they were having a silent conversation before they both looked at her again.

Mad's shoulders slumped, as if he were resigned in whatever he was about to say. "I'd *like* it to be more," he said, though he sounded like admitting it out loud had been tough for him.

Wild rubbed a hand over the back of his head. "I don't know what to say."

"Say the truth," she encouraged.

Sparing another look at Mad, who nodded at him, Wild dropped his hands and said, "I'm definitely attracted to you. But it's weird for me to say I would want to pursue more now that I know Mad wants to."

"Why is it weird?" she asked.

"Well, I don't want to...I mean...I don't want to, like, *steal* you from him."

Mad snorted. "Think pretty highly of yourself, huh, buddy?"

"Fuck," Wild groaned as he ran his hands over his face. "I knew this was going to come out all fucked up. I just mean I don't want anyone to feel like they have to choose."

"I don't want that either," Jaz was quick to interject. "That's why I suggested we *all* date. The three of us."

"Yeah, I don't think so." Wild turned to Mad. "I love ya, man, but there's no fucking way I'm dating you."

"Back at ya," Mad said.

"You guys hang out more than any couple I've ever known. Why is this such an off-putting concept?"

"Oh, I don't know. Maybe because neither of us is gay." Mad banged his water bottle down on the counter and stalked toward the coffee machine. The anger was radiating off him in waves, and Jaz began feeling all of the confidence she'd infused into herself this morning begin to wane.

"I didn't say you were," she replied, her voice quiet.

Maddox grabbed his coffee mug and took a large sip. "Sure sounded like it."

Jaz took a deep breath. "I don't think you guys are sexually attracted to one another. But I do think you're emotionally connected enough to be able to handle something like I'm suggesting."

Wild laughed, but there was no humor in it. "What does that even mean?"

Letting her arms rise and fall back at her sides in frustration, Jaz tried to think of the best way to phrase it herself. "You two know one another inside and out. You're best friends, but you're more than that too."

Maddox opened his mouth to reply, but she held up a hand to stop him.

"I'm not saying you're into one another romantically or anything like that. But you understand each other on a level most people who *are* in a relationship never experience. And I think that could make us all perfectly suited to get what we all want."

"And what is it," Wild began, "that you think we want?"

Jaz couldn't help the tears that began to prickle her eyes, though she wasn't sure why. "Me," she replied. "And I want you, both of you, if that wasn't clear." She looked at them, saw them shutting down, and became desperate, frantic, to stop it. "This *can* work. If anyone can figure it out, we can. Nothing much would even change between us, except we'd get more nights like last night. It could be great."

She moved her eyes between them, knowing what they were going to say before either of them opened their mouth. "It can work," she said again, her voice small.

Both men looked at her, but it was Maddox who spoke. "No," he said. "It can't."

♦♦♦♦

Maddox couldn't believe how fucked up this morning had gotten. He'd known it was probably going be awkward as hell and would take a few days for them to decide the best course of action was to pretend it never happened and pick up with their friendship. Clearly, Wild had been on board with that plan, but then Jaz had burst in and messed everything up.

Watching her struggle not to crumble as his words hit home was hard. Really fucking hard, and Mad almost wanted to take them back, but he knew he couldn't. He wasn't even sure what her proposition would entail, but he knew enough to be sure it wouldn't work for him. He couldn't *date* Wild. And he couldn't date a woman who was also dating his best friend. It was...weird.

"I could never date this guy," Wild said, the joke in his voice clear.

Mad appreciated that he was trying to get them back to a better place, even if Maddox thought it was useless.

"Totally not my type." Wild winked at Jaz, but the gesture fell flat.

"I'm not... I'm not..." Jaz cleared her throat. "I'm not saying you should date each other. I'm saying you could both date me, and we could just spend time all together. As a unit. Just like we've been doing since we met."

"And we'd...what? Share you?" Mad asked, unable to keep the irritation out of his voice. "Draw straws on who gets to sleep with you at night? What you're asking...it could never work."

"But it does work. People do make it—"

"Not me," Mad interrupted. "I'm sorry, Jaz. But I'm just not that guy."

Wild remained silent, and Mad would've given anything to know what he was thinking. He had to agree. Didn't he? But then why the hell wasn't he backing Mad up? Why was he letting Maddox look like the bad guy?

Jaz quickly swiped at her cheek before squaring her shoulders. "Okay. It was worth a shot, right?" she said with a smile that didn't come close to reaching her eyes.

It made Mad's chest constrict.

"I'll, um... I'll see you guys at work."

"Wait, Jaz, you don't have to—" Wild started.

"No, I do." She flashed them both another small smile for their benefit, not hers, before making her way out of the kitchen. They heard the front door close a few seconds later.

Wild let out a deep breath and bent over the counter. "That...could have gone better."

Could it have? Maddox wasn't sure. Short of her never bringing any of it up to begin with, Mad wasn't sure how that discussion could've gone any differently. Maddox took a sip of his coffee and mirrored Wild's stance. "Would've been nice if you'd had my back in all that..."

Wild's head shot up. "What the hell do you mean? I had your back." His tone was steeled with defensiveness, which made the hair on the back of Mad's neck stand up.

Mad wasn't a fan of conflict—not anymore—and he especially hated it with Wild. It had his gut clenching and his heart pounding. But he couldn't back down from it either. His frustration over the whole ordeal was beginning to feel like a runaway train, and the only way to stop it was to crash into something else or let himself derail completely. “Bullshit,” Mad bit out. “You let me do all the heavy lifting in that conversation.”

“I said I wasn’t interested. What more was I supposed to say?”

“You said you weren’t interested in dating *me,* but you weren’t so quick to say no to what she was suggesting.”

“Isn’t that what she was suggesting?” Wild was standing straight up now, his hands on his hips.

“Stop playing dumb, Wilder. I’m not in the fucking mood.”

Wild barked out a laugh, but it was incredulous and hard instead of the usual mirth it typically had. “Are you fucking serious right now? Who is in the fucking mood for this shit? Not me, that much I can tell you.” Wild was breathing hard and glaring daggers at Mad. “You know, you can blame me for the clusterfuck this turned into all you want, but that doesn’t erase your part in things.”

“No shit it doesn’t erase my part in it. I’m the one who made her run out of here.”

Wild shook his head. “That’s not what I’m talking about. Being a dickhead today won’t erase that you made out with Jaz last night. And it doesn’t erase the fact that you got off on watching *me* make out with her too.”

“I was drunk,” Mad said, the words sounding unconvincing even to his own ears.

Wild’s eyes flashed with something that looked damned close to disappointment. “You may be able to lie to a lot of people and get away with it, Mad. Even yourself." He moved to the threshold of the kitchen. "But not me. And you damn well know it." With that, Wild left Maddox standing alone, wondering how everything went to hell so fast.

CHAPTER TWELVE

The next few days were predictable in their awkwardness, but Wild couldn't blame only Maddox for it. He was just as much at fault as Mad was. Wild had always prided himself on being a fun-loving guy, the dude who was up for whatever, whenever. But that openness seemed to end with sharing a girl with his best friend. He could definitely see how someone could be attracted to multiple people at once, but the idea of exploring that option openly had never crossed his mind before Jasmine had brought it up. And there was no way he could make a move without Mad being comfortable with the idea.

Plus, Wilder felt uncomfortable too, but that was mainly because he didn't know how he *should* feel. He hadn't given it much thought—hadn't had *time* to—before Maddox made his disgust with the situation clear. And if Wild had tried to convince him otherwise, it would've seemed like he was siding with Jaz. That was definitely not the way to get things back to normal.

So the past few days had consisted of the three of them keeping their relationship professional for the most part. They stayed in their respective lanes, with Maddox and Wilder managing the gym and training clients and Jasmine teaching some of the new classes, which meant that for much of the day, Jaz wasn't even in the main part of the building.

Wild popped over a few times a day to see how things were going, talking to some of the new members, who all seemed pleased with the class offerings and instructors.

He'd talked to Jaz too, but their interactions had been short and businesslike for the most part. By the third day, Wild couldn't take it.

"You wanna grab something to eat at that new place down the street?" he asked, hopeful that she'd been waiting for an olive branch and would eagerly grab it.

"I have some things to get done around here, but thanks for the offer."

"Of course," he said. "What things, though? Your next class isn't until three thirty."

"Just some social media posts and pictures and stuff. Trying to get the word out about the yoga classes since they haven't been as filled as I'd hoped by now. I'm not sure people see this place as a yoga studio, so I'm working on ways to expand the gym's branding so it fits with the new classes." Jasmine looked up from the laptop she'd been working on, and he could sense her frustration, though he wasn't sure if it was due to the entire situation or the fact that he'd put her on the spot by asking her to lunch. He felt a pang of guilt at the thought that he might have added to what was already an awkward work environment for her.

Wild nodded as if he understood, but he didn't. Not really. This was Jasmine's chance to move things toward how they'd been before, and she wasn't taking it. "You sure you can't take a forty-five-minute break?" He plopped himself down across from her at the small table where she was working and raised an eyebrow at her. "I'll eat carbs if you go with me," he whined playfully.

"I really can't."

"Fine. I'll add in dessert, but that's my final offer."

"Wilder, please."

"Please what, Jaz?" He threw his arms out to the side. "It's not a fucking date or anything. It's just lunch. We're friends, remember?" He hadn't expected the rejection to cause such a visceral reaction in him, but he probably should have. Wild *felt* more than he *thought*; he always had. And much of the time, his responses were a direct result of that with little time spent filtering his words or emotions.

"I can't be friends with you after what happened."

"Why the hell not? This shit is stupid. We had so much fun together."

Jasmine let out a sigh, and for a moment, he thought he'd won. Not that this was an argument he wanted to win necessarily. Because for him to win, Jasmine had to lose. And the thought of her losing something else made his heart ache. He just wanted the end result to be that they could start hanging out again, and whatever means it took to get to that end would have to be worth it.

"I know we had fun together. But do you really think you and I could go somewhere together and *not* feel something more? That attraction won't go away, Wild. At least it won't for me. It'll just be too awkward."

Wild knew that was true for him too. Even after what

happened last weekend, he still fantasized about her, imagined what it would be like to take things further than they had on the dance floor. There was little chance he could suppress that curiosity permanently. He'd always wonder what it would be like to have her. "Yeah," he said, his voice surprisingly sad. "Me either."

"So why do that to ourselves, then?" she asked. "Why torture ourselves just to have a friendship when we obviously want more than that?"

It was a valid question. And one that Wild didn't have the slightest idea how to answer.

♦♦♦♦

Closing his eyes, Maddox adjusted his headphones and leaned back on the chair. Not a cloud in the sky, it was one of the most beautiful days of the entire summer. And there was no better place to spend it than alone at the pool. He'd only been there a little over an hour, and he already felt more relaxed. Nothing felt like summer more than Zac Brown Band and the heat of the sun's rays on his already tan skin. There was no doubt he could use the time away from the gym. The stress of trying to gain new members and paying for the renovation had him up almost nightly.

He told himself it would take time to get clients interested in the new class offerings, but once they did, he hoped word of mouth would take care of the rest. Wild had assured him that the addition would be an investment that would pay off in the long run. He just wished he knew how long that run was. They weren't even bringing in enough additional money to justify hiring the two new trainers.

And with that thought came one he'd been desperately trying to force out of his mind: Jasmine. He'd tried to be friendly—maybe overly so now that he thought about it—but none of his kind gestures seemed to do anything to dissolve the tension between them. He'd stopped on the way to work to get her a coffee the other day, and since he thought it would look strange to only bring one for her, he'd gotten one for Wild too. Then when he remembered that there were two other trainers who had early PT clients, he'd grabbed coffees for them as well.

"What's the occasion?" Wild asked when he saw Mad struggling with the door while bringing in six coffees.

"Thanks for the help, asshole," Maddox joked once he finally made it inside without any third-degree burns.

"It was fun watching you. Sorry," Wild said with a laugh. "Seriously, though. Why are you bringing everyone coffee?"

"I'm just in a good mood," Mad lied.

Wild looked skeptical, causing Maddox to remember Wild's words about knowing when Mad was lying, which made him feel like shit. "Okay, so I'm *trying* to get into a good mood, and I thought cheering *other* people up might be a good first step."

Not that Maddox knew how to get into a good mood, since he was a stressed, uptight asshole on a good day—something Wild had always had difficulty relating to even though he understood why Mad was the way he was. He doubted things that Wild had complete faith in—like the gym gaining revenue after the renovation or the rugby team they played for winning the championship—and Mad was the one who was correct more times than not. But what he wanted more than being right was for things not to be so weird between him and his best friend, so he gave Wild a smile that was genuine in its affection for the man who meant the world to him. Though he knew chances were better that both Jasmine and Wild recognized his random acts of kindness for what they really were.

"Well, thanks," Wild said, returning the smile.

It seemed neither of them had any more words to keep the moment going, which depressed Mad more than he'd ever let show. It frustrated him that he couldn't fix things between them. Between *all* of them.

Frustrated that he'd allowed the drama to invade his pool day, he pulled his headphones out and stood to put them under his towel with his phone. A swim would definitely help take his mind off things.

♦♦♦♦

Jasmine had noticed Maddox almost as soon as she'd arrived at the pool. She shouldn't have been surprised to see him there, since he'd been the one to tell her about it in the first place, but she kind of was. From what she could tell, he hadn't seen her yet. Of course, she didn't think he would've been in any hurry to say hello even if he had. He'd been acting crazy ever since their little talk in the guys' apartment last weekend. And by crazy she meant ignoring her and then becoming overly nice. He smiled at people for the hell of it, and he'd even offered to help one of the other trainers clean up the equipment he'd used with one of his personal training clients. It was freakin' weird, and she didn't know how much more she could take of it.

Which was why as soon as Maddox finished swimming the million laps he was doing, she planned to talk to him. She needed to make this right, needed to have things as close to back to normal as they could get. They could be attracted to each other and still be friends. Sure, she'd told Wild the opposite, but it wasn't the truth. After she'd had a couple days to think about it, she realized that even though it would certainly be tough to hang out with the two sexy men, it wasn't impossible. People did that all the time. And having a platonic relationship with Mad and Wild definitely beat not having a relationship with them at all.

Grabbing her belongings, Jasmine stood and made her way to the other side of the pool closer to where Maddox's chair was. She placed her things a few chairs down from his and continued to watch him swim, like some sort of aquatic stalker. His tan skin fit tightly over the muscles in his back, which flexed with each stroke. Maddox's movements were fluid like the water itself, and it didn't seem like he ever tired. The man was truly a machine.

Finally, he stopped at the other end of the pool and leaned against the side. Jaz wondered when, if at all, Maddox would see her and if she'd be able to recognize it when he did. She watched him for a few minutes, but he gave no indication that he'd seen her. When he began swimming again, she prepared herself for his exit out of the water, which she was certain would be one of the hottest things she'd seen in recent memory.

And it didn't disappoint. A few seconds later, Maddox's head emerged from the water, and he placed both hands on the deck of the pool as he pushed himself up. In Jasmine's mind, the moment played out in slow motion—each bead of water dropping off his hair and skin lazily until it splashed silently onto the ground. The man looked like he was cut from stone, every inch of him hard and defined. He wiped a hand over his face to get some of the water off and began walking toward his chair.

She'd come over here so easily, but now that she was faced with...facing Maddox, she felt like her presence here would seem too convenient, even though it had been a complete coincidence that she'd chosen to use the trial pass for today. He'd probably think she was there to rope him into some sort of freaky threesome he wanted no part of. She'd barely spoken to him since their morning-after chat, and though she missed their easy conversation and how Maddox had seemed so open with her, she had no idea what to say now that he was only a few feet away.

But it turned out she didn't need to. Because without even noticing she was there, Maddox found his place back in his chair and closed his eyes. She watched him for a moment, the muscles in his face relaxing and his chest rising slowly with each breath. He looked peaceful. And the last thing she wanted to do was be the one to ruin that.

She'd already ruined so much else.

CHAPTER THIRTEEN

Yoga classes weren't exactly Mad's scene, but he couldn't actually say that for sure because this was the first one he'd ever been to. He'd promised Jasmine weeks ago that he'd observe one of her classes and give her some honest feedback, and though fulfilling that promise was now awkward as fuck, he was a man of his word. And he could definitely keep his business and personal life separate.

Until he'd arrived in the room, he hadn't considered how weird it would be to watch her class without actually *taking* the class, even though that was what he'd originally planned to do. That way he wouldn't make a fool of himself or have to let Jaz help him get himself unstuck from whatever position he wound up in. But now that he was faced with the decision, he felt he couldn't just sit in the back in a chair and look on as members of his gym contorted themselves into cats or camels. So he grabbed one of the extra mats and found a space on the wood floor closer to the side of the room in the second row. He felt like maybe that spot would make it seem like he was somewhere between wanting to get a good view of the instruction and being as unobtrusive as possible. It made him feel like he was picking the seat in his first class as a college freshman—wanting to make a good impression without becoming the target of the professor's attention, especially since, at twenty-five, he'd been significantly older than the other students in his class.

Jasmine smiled at him when he'd entered and thanked him for coming as if she hadn't been sure he would. It made him feel like shit, but he wasn't sure that anything he could've done would've made her think differently.

The first thing Mad noticed was that the turnout for the class was larger than it had been since Jaz had begun teaching it, which he took as a good sign. With sixteen people there, the room was nearly at capacity. She'd begun the class with some breathing exercises on their backs, and after a few minutes, Maddox felt himself begin to unwind—as if his body and mind seemed to melt into the mat. The tension left his jaw, and his open hands felt light. Jasmine's voice floated through the studio, the soft tones mingling with the low music playing in the background.

He'd never really noticed her voice before now—how soothing her pentameter could be and how every syllable felt heavy with importance. He wondered if it was the class that had his senses heightened or the fact that it simply gave him a chance to appreciate Jasmine in a way he hadn't since the night they'd hooked up. Images of their dance—and their kiss—filled his mind, and he tried desperately to push his thoughts to the side. *Recognize any errant thoughts and move on,* as Jaz had instructed the class to do. But it was an impossible task. There was no way Maddox could think of anything *but* Jasmine in this setting, and he couldn't help but wonder if she was thinking of him too.

Had she looked at him at all since the class began? Or had she avoided even a glance in his direction? He had no idea, and it scared him how much it mattered what she thought of him. Because as much as Maddox hated to admit it, he had a thing for this woman, and whatever that thing was wouldn't go away. He told himself it was a crush, a sexual attraction that would lessen with time until it eventually disappeared completely. But even as he tried to convince himself of that, he knew he was lying.

The majority of the class passed without the need for Jasmine to interact with Maddox, but when she helped them stabilize themselves into some position that he'd already forgotten the name of, Jaz made her way through the room, subtly correcting people's positions so that they were individually challenging. Mad knew he was trying too hard, forcing himself into a static place where he feared he might be stuck for all of eternity. There were people in the room more than twice his age who were able to hold themselves for minutes in a place that Maddox knew he wouldn't be able to come close to mirroring.

"Relax your shoulder blades," Jasmine said, approaching him from behind and placing a hand on his upper back. "Reach over with your body, not only your arm. Like you're opening yourself up from your core."

Maddox wished he knew what the hell she was talking about. In theory, he did. But putting her suggestions into practice was a different story entirely. He felt tight all over, rigid in a way he knew was the opposite of yoga's purpose.

When he didn't adjust his stance, Jasmine spoke. "May

I?" she asked, touching her fingertips to his chest.

"Sure," he nearly grunted out.

Then she pulled gently on his chest, pressing his back against her body and pulling his arm over farther than he would've ever been able to get it on his own. "Like you're a fan," she said. "It's not just the blades moving. It's the whole mechanism."

The analogy made sense to Maddox, and he said, "Don't move, though, or this fan's gonna fall over."

He heard her laugh but unfortunately couldn't see it in the position he was in. She remained there for support until she directed them to stand up slowly, which, to his embarrassment, she helped him do.

After Jaz had attended to Maddox, he'd noticed her do the same with a few other people, though they definitely didn't need as much help as he did. There seemed to be a variety of ages and experience levels, but none of them looked like it was their first class. Most of the class kept up relatively well with Jasmine's directions, and with some concentration, Maddox was able to as well. Only twice did he mix up his left and right legs, but he corrected it before Jasmine noticed. He knew his left from right, but the whole thing was so overwhelming to him, he had trouble keeping up.

By the time the class was winding down, Maddox's muscles were more fatigued than he'd expected them to be. He didn't go into the class thinking yoga was an easy exercise by any means, but he definitely hadn't anticipated feeling like this. After class, he took a few minutes to introduce himself to the new members and watched as Jasmine interacted with many of them. She didn't seem to know them well necessarily, and that didn't surprise him since it was one of her first yoga classes. But she had a way of making a personal connection with each of them—asking how their knee was feeling, if they'd had a good trip to the beach this past weekend.

Once everyone had left, Maddox approached her. "That was some workout." He wiped some sweat from his forehead.

"You thought so?" Jasmine's voice rose like she was excited at the comment, and he figured it was probably much more of a compliment to her than he'd realized.

"I definitely broke a sweat. I'm a strong guy, but I couldn't hold most of those poses for more than a few seconds. And some of them I couldn't get into at all."

"Yoga's a different kind of strong," she explained, and he couldn't be sure if her comment was said for the purpose of providing information or making him feel better. "There are plenty of people who can lift a ton of weight but have trouble with even beginner yoga."

Jasmine busied herself with wiping down some of the mats that belonged to the gym, and Maddox was suddenly aware that he was standing there watching her. "Let me give you a hand," he said before moving toward the wipe dispenser and grabbing a few.

"So what do I need to fix?" she asked. She didn't sound discouraged but rather eager to hear his recommendations.

It was definitely a welcome change from other employees who hated to hear any sort of criticism, even during their formal evaluations. But now that he was standing in front of someone who valued his opinion—*asked* for it, even—he couldn't think of a damn thing to say other than, "Nothing. I think you're great."

She smiled at him and, looking almost embarrassed, said, "Come on, Maddox. There's gotta be something."

"No, seriously. I loved it."

She was quiet for a moment, her eyes locking with his in a way that seemed like she was studying the truth in them. "'Kay," she said finally before turning to put the rest of the mats back.

"What?"

"Nothing."

"It's something," Maddox insisted.

She squared herself to him, crossing her arms and waiting for him to speak. When he didn't, she said, "I don't believe you."

"Why wouldn't you believe me?"

"Because there's no way Maddox Gibson is going to sit through an hour-long class with a new trainer and not have at least one suggestion."

"Well, that's exactly what I just did."

There was a rigidity to Jasmine's jaw that Maddox noticed, and it made him uncomfortable in a way he couldn't identify. Why did everything this woman did seem to elicit some sort of physical reaction in him?

"I know," she said, sounding irritated. And though he didn't really understand why, he was hoping she might tell him. She looked like she was about to speak again, but shaking her head, she dropped her arms and turned toward the door. Then she said, "I'll just get Wild to do it."

The words stung more than they probably should have—

and certainly more than she'd meant for them to—but given what had happened between all of them, the last thing he wanted was for Jasmine to go to Wild because Mad couldn't be counted on to do something he'd promised to do. The problem was that Maddox honestly didn't have any suggestions. She was a professional and knew more about yoga than he did.

"I don't have any criticism for you. You don't have to go to Wild for it," he said sternly.

"Look," Jasmine said, sounding calmer than she had only a moment ago. She played with the knot at the bottom of her tank top—pulling it tighter as she spoke. "The last thing I wanted was to cause a problem between you and Wild."

He realized that his comment about not going to Wild had probably been misinterpreted. He just didn't want her thinking he was placating her by telling her she was a good yoga teacher. "There's no problem between Wild and me." It was the truth. He and Wilder hadn't exactly talked about anything Jasmine-related since she'd left their apartment that day, but they were best friends. Bros before hos and all that. Not that Jasmine was a ho. Just because she liked both of them didn't mean she was promiscuous. The way she'd explained it had actually made sense. Logically, at least. And also if it had applied to someone other than Maddox. But there was simply no way he could get on board with the idea. "The whole thing just weirded us out a little bit. Not that *you're* weird," he said quickly. "It's just not for us, that's all."

"You already said all this."

"I know."

Then, without speaking, they stared at each other, the air

between them thickening with every silent second that passed.

"What's the craziest thing you've ever done?" Jaz asked him. There was a light in her eyes—a glimmer of something that excited him in a way he couldn't remember feeling. Combine that with the curl to her lip, and there was no way he couldn't answer.

"Good crazy or bad crazy?"

She shrugged. "Crazy's crazy, right?"

Maddox let out a long sigh as he warred with himself. For a reason he couldn't explain, he'd wanted so badly to tell her about that time in his life, because she had a light to her that would brighten even the darkest moment in his life just by sharing it. But another part of him worried about what she might say—or rather what she might *think* of him. That he was weak or selfish. And the last thing Maddox wanted was for the woman he cared so much for to think less of him.

But something told him that no matter what he revealed to Jasmine, it wouldn't change her opinion of him. So before he could chicken out, he said, "I tried to kill myself." Saying the words out loud was strange—considering he'd never told another person, not even Wild. Though he'd assumed Wild always suspected what Mad was up to when they met on top of the bridge, Mad staring at the depths below, they'd never spoken of it after Wild had convinced Mad to join him for dinner. The rest had been history, and Mad had never wanted to bring it up. Had never wanted to confirm just how big a mess he'd been when he'd been discharged from the army with nowhere to go and no skills to fall back on.

Jasmine's lips parted, but she didn't speak. Maddox was grateful for it.

"Wild stopped me," he added. "It's how we met, actually." He almost expanded on the story, but Jaz's expression prevented it. She looked like she might cry, like she was surely regretting asking the question, and it made Mad's throat dry up. "Sorry," he said, shaking his head. He reached up to tug on his hair a bit but thought better of it because he figured the gesture would probably make Jasmine think he was even more insane. "I'm sure that wasn't what you had in mind when you asked that."

"No," she said. "I'm the one who should be sorry. I didn't mean for you to think of that. It must be such a painful memory. I had no idea."

"How could you?" Mad wasn't sure when they'd gotten closer or who had entered whose space, but they were close enough now for him to smell the soap on her skin, the coconut and mint of her hair. She smelled like fucking summer, and he couldn't breathe in enough of her.

"Can I ask why you did it?" she said, her voice so quiet, so cautious, that if they weren't as close as they were, he probably wouldn't have heard her.

"Because I was fucked up," he explained. "I'm *still* fucked up."

He didn't resist when she took his hand, and he wasn't sure if it was just because he welcomed the comfort or because it went against his every instinct to reject any type of physical contact from her.

"I think everyone is *some* kind of fucked up," she said.

They were both quiet for a long time, and Maddox wondered if she could hear how fast his heart was beating. "I can't be who you want me to be," he said at last.

She put a hand up to touch his cheek. Her touch was soft, slow, like she was scared the action might startle him. "I think you already are," she whispered.

Maddox put a hand over hers and brought it down to their sides before releasing it. "You know what I mean," he said. "I want you, Jaz. I think that's pretty obvious. But I can't be a guy who looks the other way while you screw my best friend."

"I never said you had to turn around." She laughed, but it faded when she realized her attempt at humor didn't land. "I'm kidding."

"Are you, though? I mean, really." He took a few steps back, suddenly needing the space. His mind was so fucking jumbled, his body so full of feeling that he didn't trust himself not to kiss her when she was that close. "How does something like that even work? Like...like one of us takes you out and then you spend the night with that person? Or we all go out and you choose one of us?" Now he pulled at his hair, not giving a fuck what it looked like. Why the hell he was even asking about this, he couldn't explain, because there was absolutely no fucking way he'd ever try it. Not a chance.

"It can work however we want it to. That's what I was trying to explain at your apartment. It'd be our relationship. Mine and yours and Wild's. There are no rules other than the ones we'd make."

"This is ridiculous," Maddox said.

"Is it? You keep saying that, but the fact that we're talking about it now—and that you were okay with it that night—"

"I was drunk!" Even though he'd already been called

out on this lie, he couldn't help it from spilling from his lips a second time.

She raised an eyebrow at him. "We both know Maddox Gibson never really gets drunk. Not drunk enough to do something he wouldn't do sober, at least."

She had a point, though he'd never admit to it.

"You want to know why I asked you what the craziest thing you ever did was?"

He paused for a moment, his arms settling over his chest and his breathing slowing some. "Why?"

She looked into his eyes in a way that made it impossible for him to look anywhere else. "I was hoping you'd realize that night with me...that night with Wild," she said, "that wasn't it."

CHAPTER FOURTEEN

Wild was sitting on the couch playing video games when Mad came in the front door and grunted, "Hey."

"What's up? Decide to stay and close up?" Wild asked. Normally, Mad would've been home hours ago. And while Mad had a life outside of Wild, the events of the past couple weeks had put Wild on edge. Which was why he was playing video games at eleven p.m. on a weeknight when he had to open the gym at five the next morning.

Plopping down on the recliner, Mad leaned back and stared at the ceiling. "Drove around for a while. I needed to think about a few things."

Wild paused the game and tossed the controller on the coffee table. "Anything you want to talk about?"

Mad let out a dry laugh before saying, "Not really. But I should anyway." After a few more seconds, he sat up straighter and looked at Wild. "Are you into Jaz? I know you said you were attracted to her, but are you actually into her? Beyond sex?"

Wild bristled at the question but struggled not to show it. Realistically, he couldn't blame Maddox for asking. Wild hadn't ever been one for long-term commitment. He liked to live impulsively, something a relationship severely hampered.

It wasn't that he *couldn't* be faithful. He just didn't have any desire to be. But Mad suggesting he was only into Jaz as far as he could hit it and quit it rankled. "Yeah. I'm into her beyond sex. Though, I mean...I'm not imagining white picket fences or any shit like that. I just mean, my feelings, they're beyond casual."

Mad sighed heavily. "Yeah. Mine too."

They sat there in silence for a moment, Wild wondering where that left them and Mad likely thinking the same.

"Could you do it?" Mad finally asked.

"Do what?" Wild asked, confused.

"Share her with me. Is that something you could really do?"

Wild thought for a second. His knee-jerk reaction was to say no because he knew that was probably what Mad wanted to hear. Maddox had probably driven around for hours questioning everything he knew about himself and come up with no answers he liked. Wild saying that he couldn't do what Jaz was asking of them would let Mad off the hook. He wouldn't have to confront the truth of what he wanted if Wild nixed the idea outright. But the hesitance was Mad's fear talking, and Wilder couldn't validate it. Wouldn't, because it wasn't the truth. "Yeah. Yeah, I think it would take some getting used to, but I don't think it would be a deal breaker for me."

Rubbing his hands over his face, Mad groaned. "I just... I don't know what I think about it. Part of me thinks it's fucking nuts to even think about, but then another part of me, the part that remembers what it was like to watch her with you at that club, isn't bothered by it. It's fucking confusing."

"Tell me this," Wild said. "When you think back on that night, is any part of you angry at me for kissing her? Did you want to pull her away from me? Push me away? Anything?"

Mad sat there a second before slowly shaking his head. "No. I think with anyone else I would've been. But with you, I dunno. We've been sharing things for almost ten years. It felt... natural to share that too. And I know it's different. That she's a person and that it's a fuck-ton more complicated than sharing a pizza or some shit. But it felt...okay."

"Just okay?" Wild prompted.

"God, you're annoying. Fine, asshole, it felt...not as awkward as I thought. Like what we were doing was totally okay."

"Maybe there's a reason for that."

Mad snorted. "Or maybe this is a fucked-up situation destined to go FUBAR at any moment."

Laughing, Wild said, "That's possible too. But we won't know if we don't try. And Mad? I want to try. I think we'll always regret it if we don't." He said it with conviction, knowing Mad needed at least one of them to be sure.

"It can't mess up our friendship, Wild. I can lose a lot of things, but you're not one of them."

"If you think you're ever getting rid of me, you've lost your goddamn mind."

"I can't believe I'm going to do this," Mad muttered.

"I don't know why. I've convinced you to do all sorts of shit over the years." Wild hoped his joke would break some of the tension in the room and was relieved when Mad laughed.

"I can't... I don't want people to know, though," Mad said.

"Does that make me an asshole?"

"I think it makes you a responsible business owner. Which one of us has to be, and we both know it can't be me."

Maddox laughed again and stood. "Okay. Let's go get our girl."

Wild leaped up, a spring in his step as he followed Mad out to his car so they could do just that.

Jaz lay in bed and scrolled through Instagram, trying to will herself to be tired. Most of the time, looking at the screen helped tire her eyes out. Probably not the healthiest way to fall asleep, but effective. Usually. After her talk with Maddox—and the bombshell he'd dropped on her—he'd excused himself without saying anything more.

She couldn't picture Mad contemplating suicide. The very thought of it made her chest ache. And while she was nearly desperate to know the story there, she also knew she'd never ask. If Mad wanted to share more with her, she'd listen with open ears and an open heart. But if not, then she was just going to have to accept that.

Unable to resist, she went to Wild's Instagram page. Mad didn't have one, but he didn't really need one with the presence he had on Wild's page. She swiped through picture after picture, focusing on the ones featuring both of them. Her eyes began to sting as she thought about how much she wanted to be part of that. Part of *them*. She wanted to make goofy faces with Wild as she hung off Mad's arm: the storm and the rock. Though with the new information she'd learned today, they clearly switched roles from time to time. And she could see it. As she thought back over the time she'd known them, she recognized how Mad leaned on Wild and how Wild remained solid for his friend.

Wild was impulsive and chaos incarnate, but at his core he was steady, consistent. She'd called him a study in contrasts, and she hadn't been kidding. What she hadn't realized was how much Mad was the same. His constant control was clearly something hard-earned—and perhaps something he lost from time to time.

She sighed as she continued to look through Wild's feed. A loud banging on her door caused her to startle, dropping her phone on the comforter and sitting up quickly. Her heart rate kicked up a few thousand notches as she stared at the doorway of her bedroom. The banging came again, but this time she could also make out voices. Voices that seemed to be yelling at one another.

Her phone dinged with an alert. *It's us. I told Wild to stop banging on your door, but he's a dumbass. Can you let us in? Also, sorry if we woke you up.* The text from Mad had her springing out of bed and running to the front door. She unlocked the deadbolt and slid open the chain before throwing the door open to reveal the two most beautiful men she'd ever seen. Not that she'd say that out loud. "Do you two know how to tell time?"

"Did we wake you?" Wild asked.

"Well, no, but—"

"Then stop making a big deal out of nothing," Wild said with a teasing grin. "Can we come in?"

She stepped back, and the two men walked past her, Mad giving her a lingering look that nearly melted the panties off her body. Thank God she had on sleep shorts. “So, not that I don’t love late-night surprises, but do you guys want to tell me what you’re doing here?” she asked, willing her voice to not sound hopeful. But come *on.* It was after eleven thirty on a weeknight. This had to mean something. Right?

Mad rubbed a hand over his close-cropped hair. “I’m not sure where to start.”

Wild rolled his eyes. “For Christ’s sake. Let’s not make this more complicated than we already have. We want to do the thing. That you said. Or we want to try, at least.”

Jaz’s heart leaped at his words, but she forced herself to remain calm. “Can you be more specific about the, um, *thing* you’re referring to?”

Wild opened his mouth, but Mad’s next words cut him off. “Dating. We would both like to...date you. If that’s still something you want?”

“Yeah.” Her voice sounded breathless, but she didn’t have it in her to care. “Yeah, I still want that.”

“Thing is,” Mad continued. “I’m not sure I can do it the way you saw it. I can maybe get over the fact that you’re also hanging out with Wild, but I’m not sure I can be there to watch it. It’s...weird to me. For all of us to go out on a date, I mean. I think I need the separation. Is that... Would that work for you?”

Jaz wanted to yell that she’d take them any way she could have them, but she didn’t want to seem eager like a child on Christmas morning. She had to play this cool. “Whatever you're comfortable with. I do think it's important that we keep the lines of communication open, make sure everyone is aware of how things are going. And we have to promise one another that we'll be honest about how we're feeling. I don't think this can work otherwise."

"Yeah, that makes sense," Wild agreed. "I mean, I'm not sure we need to get into specifics about our relationships. But a general idea of how we're all doing is a good idea."

Mad cleared his throat. "In the interest of being honest, I want to say that I may royally suck at this. I can count the number of serious relationships I've had on one hand. I tend to fuck things up when I'm dealing with a more...traditional relationship. I'm not sure I'll fare any better at this. But I want to try."

"None of us has been in a position like this before. We're all going to have allow for a pretty steep learning curve, I think," Jaz said. Though she had explored the concept of polyamory, she didn't have any firsthand experience. Something she hoped to rectify now.

"And if it's not working, then we need to be honest about that," Wild said, his voice firm. "If shit starts going downhill, we have to put a stop to it before we fuck up our friendships. I'm all for experimenting and having some fun and seeing where this attraction can take us, but not at the expense of our friendships. I won't risk that."

Jaz wasn't sure she liked Wild calling what they were about to embark on an "experiment" or "some fun." In her mind, it was going to be a helluva lot more than that. But she didn't want to spook him. It was better to let things grow organically than to try to force her image of how things should be onto them. Especially since she didn't really *know* how things should be. "I agree," she said simply. "So, what do we do now?"

Everyone laughed, Jaz included.

"How about you and I start with dinner tomorrow night?" Mad said.

"Yeah, and there's a new place that's basically an arcade for adults we could go to. Maybe Friday?" Wild asked her, sounding like someone had just told him he could have a puppy. They were both looking at her expectantly, hope radiating from each of them.

There was so much at risk here but so much to gain as well. And Jaz was a glass-half-full kinda girl. "I say let's do it."

CHAPTER FIFTEEN

Maddox surreptitiously tugged at his collar, trying to loosen the knot of his tie a bit. Jesus, was it hot in here or was it just him? He glanced around the upscale French restaurant, feeling as though eyes were on him. He felt like he stuck out like a sore thumb—like everyone there knew he was pretending to be sophisticated and failing miserably.

The waiter brought them a bottle of sparkling water, handed Maddox a wine list, and reviewed the specials before saying he'd give them a moment to look over the wine selection. Maddox watched the guy walk away as if he had clouds strapped to his feet, floating to the next table with an elegant air about him that made Mad feel even more out of place. Feeling bested by the waiter did not bode well for the rest of the evening.

Mad's gaze darted to Jaz, who looked stunning in a burgundy strapless dress. She looked amazing. "Do you prefer red or white wine?" he asked, skimming the wine selection like he knew what the hell he was looking at.

"You choose," Jaz said. The hesitance in her voice made him look up at her. She was scanning the restaurant, taking it all in, her eyes a bit wide. When she let her gaze settle back on him, she said, "Can I ask you something?"

"Anything," he replied, surprised that he meant it.

"Why are we here?"

Maddox startled a bit at her question and then set down the black book with the drinks in it. "Because I asked you to dinner and you said yes."

"No, I know that. I mean why are we *here*?"

"Is there somewhere else we should be?" he asked, confused.

"Yes. Like maybe somewhere I can actually read the menu." Her lips kicked up at the corners as she spoke. "This place is nice. More than nice, it's beautiful. But it's not...us."

Mad inhaled sharply at her words, taken aback by her referring to them as an "us." Granted, he knew they were on a date and therefore logically constituted an "us," but there was more to it than that. More in her tone that made him feel that they were an actual unit, a pairing that wasn't simply seeing if they were compatible but that compatibility was a foregone conclusion. It both thrilled and scared him.

Just as Mad opened his mouth to answer her, the waiter returned. "Have you chosen a wine to accompany your meal, or would you like me to recommend something?"

Mad stared at the man as his brain tried to think of what to say. Frustration began to bubble up in him as his desire to impress Jaz ran smack into the reality that he clearly didn't have the ability to do that. His mind seemed to scramble, making it impossible for him to pick out a coherent thought in the melee. He looked over at Jaz, sure he was going to see embarrassment all over her face because her date was evidently fucking incapable of ordering a bottle of wine.

But that was not what he saw.

When their gazes collided, he saw Jaz actually relax instead of tense up. She seemed to be forcing her lips into a flat line as if she was trying to fight a smile, and the look in her eyes was amused. Was she...laughing?

Oddly enough, it was exactly what he needed. This posh fucking restaurant, with its robotic servers and upper-crust clientele, wasn't his scene—wasn't *either* of their scenes. And Mad didn't have to be embarrassed by not fitting in there, because he didn't *want* to fit in there. It wasn't anything against the people enjoying their meals, but like Jaz had said, it wasn't them. And he didn't want it to be.

Jaz tilted her head slightly and looked up at the waiter. "I think we need a few more minutes."

The waiter nodded and began to back away, but Mad stopped him. "Actually, I think we're going to try somewhere else. Thanks anyway." Then Mad was out of his chair and pulling Jaz's out so she could stand as well. They wasted no time walking toward the exit and out onto the street.

As soon as they hit the sidewalk, Jaz faced skyward and inhaled deeply before turning to Maddox and smiling widely at him. "Thank God you got us out of there. I was worried they were going to sneak snails into my food or something."

Maddox laughed. "Sorry about that. Not sure what I was thinking."

She put a hand on his arm and looked up at him in a way that Mad could only call adoringly. "You were thinking that you wanted to impress me, and I'm flattered and appreciative. But promise me you'll never do it again."

Maddox laughed again, grabbing the hand that was on

his arm and threading their fingers together. "Noted. Is there somewhere else you'd like to eat?"

She bit the inside of her cheek and studied him. "I may have heard about a food truck festival that's happening this week on the other side of town. But if you tell Wilder, I'll call you a liar to your face."

He started moving them in the direction of his truck. "That's really where you want to go?" Maddox didn't want her to suggest something simple just because she thought he'd be more comfortable there. He wanted to make sure she enjoyed their date so that she'd want to go on more of them.

"Hell yes. Everything there is going to be so bad for us. It'll be amazing."

Maddox chuckled. "I swear, I could kiss you right now."

Jaz stopped abruptly, jerking Mad to a stop. He looked at her curiously until she said in barely more than a whisper, "You could, you know?"

Maddox turned so he was facing her and stepped closer so that their bodies were almost touching but not quite. "Could what?" he asked because he wanted to be sure, didn't want to misread a single thing, because he couldn't blow this, whatever this was, with Jaz.

"Kiss me." Her voice was low and breathy as she kept her eyes on his.

Maddox shuffled slightly closer, letting his body brush against hers. He felt her breath catch as her chest hitched against his. It felt as if everything slowed down—like one of those movies where everything races around the couple but they're being filmed in slow motion. The people walking past them, the cars whizzing by, it all blurred around them as Maddox kept his eyes on Jaz's as they both leaned toward one another.

When their lips connected, Mad's eyes slammed shut, as if he needed to shut down all of his other senses so he could immerse himself in this one. The feel of her lips, pliant beneath his, made his pulse quicken. He darted his tongue out to swipe over her bottom lip, and when she opened for him, he couldn't help but take it deeper. Bringing a hand up to cradle her jaw, Maddox let his tongue sweep into her mouth and tangle with hers, their kiss growing frenzied and passionate in milliseconds.

He knew this wasn't their first kiss, but it felt like it. The ones in the club had been driven by sexual tension and raw need. But this one was altogether different. Not because the tension and need weren't there—they sure as hell were—but there was also...more. Because they'd laid all their cards on the table already, neither of them had to wonder what this kiss meant.

It meant everything.

♦ ♦ ♦ ♦

Wild's brain was on excitement overload. Not only was he hanging out with Jaz in a capacity that was decidedly more than buddies, but also the place they were at was fucking awesome. Parker's Adult Arcade was set up in a warehouse and had everything from paintball to laser tag to ax throwing to an adult bouncy house obstacle course. It was like someone had reached into his brain, pulled out all of his favorite things, and put them all in one room. He'd have to come back here with Mad. He'd love the hell out of it.

"I can't wait to embarrass you at this," Jaz said as they waited for their time to throw the axes. She'd been making threats like that all night—telling him she was going to kick his ass in this and that. And the majority of the time, she wasn't wrong. For someone so small and pretty, she was fiercely competitive.

"You don't stand a chance. I'm practically a world champion at darts. I'm going to rock at this too."

She raised an unimpressed eyebrow. "Please. You can barely hit a piece of drywall with a sledgehammer."

Wild narrowed his eyes at her. "Have you and Maddox been talking shit about me?"

She giggled, and it made him unable to hide his smile. Man, she was fun. Wild couldn't remember the last time he'd enjoyed a date this much. And unlike Mad, who was picky about who he'd dated in the past, Wild had been on *lots* of dates—mostly first dates but dates all the same.

When it was their turn, Wild motioned like a gentleman for Jaz to go first.

Jaz scoffed. "You're the world champion. Show me what you got."

"Okay. But don't blame me when you're too embarrassed to take your turn after seeing how awesome I am."

"Just throw the damn thing."

Wilder laughed as he approached the guy holding the ax. The man gave Wild advice about how to stand and aim and then handed him an ax and got the hell out of the way. Wrapping his hands around the handle, Wild staggered his stance like he'd been instructed and stared at the target, willing himself to do well. He pulled the ax back over his head and then quickly brought his hands forward, releasing it at what he thought was precisely the right moment to split the target right down the middle.

He was wrong. So very wrong. The ax sailed wide to the right, embedding itself in the plywood for a half second before clattering to the ground. Hearing snickering behind him, he slowly turned around. "Okay, so it's a little different than darts."

Snorting out a laugh, Jaz said, "Ya think?"

"I just need to get the hang of it." He got five throws. Surely each one would get progressively better.

Spoiler alert: they didn't. He only made contact with the target once, and the ax was somehow sideways when it happened. When he stepped back to let Jaz have her turn, he tried hard to not seem like his ego had been slightly bruised by his performance.

"That was...informative. Thank you." Jaz tried, and failed, to fight a smile as she spoke.

"Yeah, yeah, let's see how you do before you talk any more smack."

After receiving the same instructions Wild had, Jaz got in position and took aim. Her throw was strong and precise, causing the ax to sail through the air and slice into the target. It wasn't a bull's-eye, but she not only managed to hit the damn thing, she managed to throw it hard enough that it stayed put. The worker pulled it free before she took her next turn. Which was even better than her first. With each throw, Jaz inched closer to a bull's-eye. She never actually got one—*thank God*—but she came damn close.

As they walked away, Wild threw his arm around her shoulders. "I feel like I got hustled."

"Would it make you feel better if I said you kinda did?"

"No. But tell me anyway."

Jaz huffed out a soft laugh before saying, "My mom's second husband used to like to go out and chop down his own firewood. He had a cabin in the mountains, and we'd go up there on weekends when we were kids. He'd disappear for hours each day and come back in sweating and hauling wood. One day I asked if I could go with him, he said sure, and we became instant chopping buddies. So while I've never thrown an ax before, I am pretty familiar with handling them."

"Is this the same guy who taught you how to put down a hardwood floor?"

"One and the same."

Wilder squeezed her shoulder. "He sounds like a great guy."

"Yeah, he was definitely my favorite."

"Favorite?" Wild asked, thinking the phrasing strange. Jaz hadn't shared much about her family. Little tidbits here and there, but she tended to be vague on the subject.

"Favorite of the stepfathers."

"How many have you had?"

"Mom will be marrying husband number five in a couple of months." Wild must not have done a good job of keeping the surprise off his face, because Jaz continued. "My mom had my older sister, Isabella, right out of high school. Her parents and his kind of forced them to get married shotgun style, and from the stories I've heard, it was truly toxic. She eventually got pregnant with me—I don't know if it was an accident or she was trying to keep him around or what—but as soon as he heard the news, he skipped off to parts unknown. He wasn't there when I was born, nor a single day since."

Jaz sighed heavily, and Wild was just about to tell her she didn't have to talk about it if she didn't want to when she began to speak again. "I think he broke something in her. I think she spent so many years trying to hold on to him that she decided she'd never try to hold on to anyone in that way again." Jaz looked up at him and gave him a small smile. "Except her girls, of course. Us she'd hang on to with shackles if she could. Anyway, it seems like she's constantly searching for her Prince Charming, marries him as soon as she thinks she's found him, but as soon as the fairy tale starts to fade, she's gone. Her second husband was around the longest because he's the father of my younger sister, Ariel, and my mom tried to stick it out with him. But ultimately, he became part of her pattern. She serves them with divorce papers and never looks back."

Wild had no idea what to say to that, so he uttered the only truth he could think of. "Sounds like a really tough life."

"Yeah," Jaz murmured. "It really is."

Wild thought about what Jaz had told him, his brain connecting her mom's story to his own. Not that they were similar because Wild never even let things get to the fairy tale stage. When he left at midnight, he was always careful to not leave any shoes behind.

Shaking the thoughts from his mind, he asked Jaz what

she'd like to do next.

Taking a moment to look around, she pointed over to an inflatable obstacle course. As they made their way over, she said, "Let's make this one interesting."

"What'd you have in mind?"

They arrived at the course, and she turned to face him, sliding her hands around his waist. "If I win, you have to kiss me."

Wild raised an eyebrow. These were terms he could get on board with. "And if I win?"

"I'll kiss you."

Wild was turned on by how brazen she was. He knew she'd kissed Maddox on their date. She'd told him almost as soon as he'd picked her up because she didn't want there to be any secrets between them. He was glad she'd been honest, but the news didn't bother him in the least. "You're on."

The two got ready to race, and when the whistle blew, everything became a blur. Wild climbed up and then slid down. He hoisted himself over things and crawled under others. And when he finally got to the end, he sent up a prayer of thanks that Jaz wasn't waiting for him. And though she wasn't far behind, that didn't stop Wild from being smug.

"Guess you win," she said.

"Guess I do."

And later that night, when he collected his kiss outside of her apartment door, pulling her to him with his lips hovering above hers as he waited for her to close the distance, Wild felt a piece click into place. He felt her lips smiling against his as she pressed them firmly together, nipping at his bottom lip, prompting him to open up for her tongue to sweep in. Usually the aggressor, it was heady for Wild to cede that to someone else. To let someone else direct the kiss as he followed her lead was everything he never knew he was missing. He let his hands drift down to cup her ass and notch her against him so that her pelvis rubbed against the hardness that was trapped in his pants. She moaned at the contact as a shiver ran up Wild's spine.

Her arms wrapped more tightly around him, causing him to literally bend to her will as he stooped to accommodate her shorter stature until he decided it would be easier to hoist her up. She wrapped her toned legs around his waist, gyrating slowly against him, the kiss frenzied as they tried to devour one another.

A throat clearing caused them to freeze with their lips still attached.

When Wild's eyes snapped open, he saw Jaz staring back at him, amusement evident in her gaze. They slowly parted, and Jaz looked down the hall at her elderly neighbor who'd made the noise as she passed. "Sorry, Mrs. Gramble," Jaz called after her.

As the woman unlocked her apartment door, she said, "Just didn't want you to get arrested for indecent exposure before you got to the good stuff," over her shoulder before disappearing and locking herself inside.

Jaz and Wild looked at one another and burst into laughter. Wild set Jaz down, though she kept her arms around him. "I had a great time tonight."

"Me too."

Jaz smiled softly. “I’ll see you at the gym tomorrow?”

“Definitely,” Wild whispered before leaning down and taking another soft kiss. Then he stepped back from her and waited for her to let herself into her apartment before adjusting himself and heading to his car. As he drove home, Wild pondered a great many things, but one thing was for certain: he’d never looked forward to a tomorrow as much as he did right then.

CHAPTER SIXTEEN

"What's your favorite kind of ice cream?" Jaz asked.

Maddox tried to remember the last time he had more than a few spoonfuls of ice cream, but he couldn't. He and Wild didn't keep it in their apartment, and he never really got dessert, even on his cheat days. But somehow he'd let Jaz convince him to go to a homemade-ice-cream shop, which was probably a mistake, because he was now plowing through a bowl of chocolate peanut butter cup drizzled with hot fudge.

He'd have to get up early to run a few extra miles tomorrow. But even though he hated running, getting to watch Jaz's tongue sweep across her cone so it didn't drip would be worth a fucking marathon if that's what it took. "Vanilla," he said.

Her eyebrows narrowed as she laughed. "Then why did you get chocolate peanut butter?"

"Oh," he said, looking down. "Yeah, this *was* my favorite. But then I started watching what you're doing to that cone, and I changed my mind."

Jasmine glanced at the vanilla on top of the sugar cone she was holding and then brought her eyes up to meet Maddox's again. Then she ran her tongue over her bottom lip to catch some of the ice cream at the corner before holding the cone up to his mouth. "I can share," she said.

The irony of her words wasn't lost on him, but he chose not to comment. The idea of sharing Jasmine hadn't bothered him yet, though he definitely tried not to think about what she may or may not be doing with Wilder. Besides, it wasn't like the three of them were out on a date together. No one sitting outside the ice cream shop knew she was dating someone else.

And more than that, he had such a good time with her—was so attracted to her—that he'd hold on to her like he was a kid trying to hold on to the string of a fucking balloon as it blew around in the breeze. So he did what he'd been doing more of lately: listened to his instincts rather than his brain. He scooted a little closer to her on the bench and leaned down to put his mouth on the ice cream she was offering him.

"Good?" she asked.

"The best," he answered. "I'm definitely on Team Vanilla now."

♦♦♦♦

Maddox's voice was low and raspy in a way that Jasmine was certain he wasn't aware of. The man had no idea how sexy he was. He didn't have the swagger or the cockiness that Wilder had, but that was part of the appeal to her. He was sure of himself in a way that seemed more intrinsic—a quiet confidence that ran through every cell in his body. She could feel it when he lifted his hand up to cup the back of her neck and pull her toward him. And when his lips touched hers, there was a lightness to the kiss that had her practically moaning with need.

She'd thought about his mouth since he'd kissed her the first time, but they hadn't done anything more yet. Jasmine wanted to take things slowly, move at a pace each man was comfortable with. But the gradual build was killing her. Images of Maddox working out with his shirt off, all sweat and heavy breathing, filled her mind as their kiss deepened to something that definitely wasn't appropriate for a family atmosphere. Maddox seemed to realize the same because the kiss became more innocent, his lips moving more slowly over hers until they stopped completely.

Biting at her lip as their foreheads touched, she could see from the way his mesh shorts tented that he was just as turned on. "We should probably just finish our ice cream," she said.

Mad cleared his throat and inhaled slowly, like he was trying to get his body under control. "Right."

They went back to sitting side by side again, their attention directed in front of them at the passing cars and the people walking by as they ate some more. When Jasmine's hand went to Mad's thigh, he said, "I think I'm done."

"Me too," Jaz said with a smile and an ache low in her core that she hoped like hell Maddox would attend to.

The only conversation they had after that was the one with their eyes. Even though Maddox shouldn't have had much of an appetite, he was looking at her like he could eat her alive. And with the thought of Maddox running his tongue all over her body, she walked with him to his truck, which was parked on a side street about a block away. But they never made it inside.

Jasmine found herself pressed against the passenger door

with Maddox's body holding her firmly in place with his hips. She'd never contemplated having sex on a residential street before, but now she was thinking just that. The thought of wrapping her legs around Mad's waist as he pounded into her had her legs practically buckling beneath her as he ground his erection slowly against her stomach.

She wasn't sure what he was willing to do, so she let him take the lead. When his mouth moved down her neck, she moved her head to give him access. And when she felt his fingers slipping beneath the hem of her tank top to graze her skin, she put her hand on his and guided it up a bit so he knew she was right there with him, desperately wanting him to take things further. And it wasn't only because she physically needed this man to touch her. She wanted to show him what he did to her, how he made her feel.

Somewhere in the back of her mind was a voice that was telling her she wished she could show Wild the same thing—wished she could show them both together. But she silenced that voice entirely, at least for now, and focused on the hand that was moving up her torso, the fingers that played with her nipple when they found their destination. The combination of Maddox's groans and his large, rough hands on her soft breasts caused parts deep inside her to contract.

She moved her hands to his ass, which was probably the most perfectly round and muscular one she'd ever felt. She dragged her nails against his skin and slipped her hand down the back of his shorts, which caused his muscles to clench and his hips to move more wildly. Moments later, she moved her hand toward his front, slowly and carefully, to make sure it was something he was comfortable with. And when she reached his cock—unbelievably thick as she took it in her hand—she felt compelled to ask, "Is this okay?"

"It's perfect," he practically grunted out. "God, I've been waiting for you to touch me like this for so fucking long."

Thoughts of Maddox fantasizing about her, maybe even touching himself to thoughts of her, had her begging him to touch her too, to put his fingers inside her until she came. And suddenly there they were, stroking each other on a public street as the sun faded over the nearby houses.

At first, she tried to keep quiet, but it wasn't long before she didn't care who heard them or who saw them. The fullness she felt from only Mad's fingers had her imagining what it would feel like to have his cock filling her instead. It felt so warm in her hand, so long. And she could feel him strain, his muscles tensing, as he told her he was going to come.

"You want me to keep going?" she whispered.

He laughed softly in her ear and said, "I'll be really disappointed if you don't."

That made her smile. "I meant more like we could do something else. If you wanted. *Go* somewhere else."

"I like what you're doing right now," he said, and when his thumb ran over her clit, she nearly let go completely.

She was so lost in sensation, so overwhelmed by Mad's fingers on her—*inside* her—and how slick the tip of his dick was from his pre-come. She moaned greedily as he thrust his fingers into her harder, stroking her in a way she would never even think of doing to herself. It made her move faster over his length, pull more frantically when she knew they were both so close.

Mad came first, come squirting from him in hot bursts that landed on the part of her stomach that was exposed due to Maddox's hand under her shirt. He groaned heavily with his orgasm, and she managed to wait until he was done, until the evidence of his pleasure began to drip down her skin before she allowed herself to find her own release. Her entire body quaked as she clenched hard around Maddox's fingers. Drawing out her orgasm with every stroke, he gradually decreased his speed until all of his movements stopped completely, and she was left feeling like she was one gigantic exposed nerve.

He moaned against her mouth when he kissed her once more before pulling back and telling her he'd find something to clean her off. He opened his back door and came out with a T-shirt. "Sorry," he said as he wiped himself from her.

"You better not be sorry," she said. "That was so hot."

Wilder nearly sprinted to the door when he heard a knock that he knew was Jasmine. But when it wasn't, he suddenly became aware that he was wearing nothing but a towel around his waist. He quickly grabbed at the top of it to make sure it held in place and raised an eyebrow at the woman currently staring at him, wide-eyed. Dark skin, high cheekbones, and glasses, with her curly hair pulled back, beautiful without a speck of makeup evident on her face. She was definitely Wilder's type, but he found himself wanting her to go away rather than invite her in. "Uh, can I help you?" he stammered, embarrassed by his lack of clothing, especially when she looked so put together in heels that revealed her red toenails and a sheer cream blouse tucked into the front of her tight dark jeans.

But somehow despite all that, she seemed more flustered than Wild was. “I think I got your mail,” she finally managed to get out.

“Oh.” Wild held out his hand, but the woman seemed to have forgotten she was supposed to hand it over and was clutching it to her chest. He smiled and then said, “I guess I’ll take my mail, then.”

“Right,” she said quickly as she extended a hand toward him, which held two envelopes. She looked at them before saying, “You must be Maddox, then.”

“Wilder, actually. Maddox is my roommate, but I’ll be sure to give him these. Thanks again,” he said, taking them.

She held on to them for what seemed to be an awkwardly long amount of time before saying, “Hope to see you around, then, Wilder. I’m Kat.” She pointed a thumb down the hall. “I just moved into 3C.”

Wilder nodded but didn’t say anything, hoping the silence would cause her to leave, which thankfully it did. But not without her saying, “Maybe we can get together sometime.”

He didn’t respond to that either, which was probably a good thing, because Jasmine appeared a moment later, and she’d no doubt heard at least some of the conversation. Not that he would’ve agreed to go out with her or anything.

“What did Kat from 3C want?” Jaz asked.

He expected her to be annoyed, jealous even. Other girls he’d dated would have been. But when he looked at her face, her expression seemed amused. There was a hint of a smile, and her eyebrow was raised in curiosity.

"She was delivering Maddox's mail."

"She's the prettiest mailman I've ever seen," Jaz teased, making Wild laugh as he ran a hand over his forehead and wet hair.

"What am I gonna do with you?"

Jaz gave him a smile that made him harden almost instantaneously. She slid her hands over his chest and up to wrap around his neck, and then she popped up on her tippy-toes and whispered into his ear, "I have a few ideas."

They'd only kissed a few times before this, and those kisses had been heated and hungry. Each time had left him with an erection he'd had to take care of himself, so the possibility of Jasmine touching him this time had his heart picking up the pace and his skin lighting up at her touch. "Do any of them involve me putting clothes on?"

"Nope," she said slowly. Then she reached down to undo his towel, kicking the door shut lightly behind her.

They made their way to the couch, their hands removing articles of clothing from Jaz's body with an urgency neither one of them had shown before. "This is...unexpected," he said in between kisses. "Though I'm not complaining."

Jaz laughed against his mouth as they collapsed on the couch with Jasmine on top of him. "Really? What did you *think* would happen if I saw you in only a towel? Kat from 3C would've jumped on it if you'd given her the green light."

"But I didn't," he said between kisses. "Only you."

She moved her hand to his dick, and he let out a low groan and closed his eyes. She began jerking him slowly, lightly, as if every stroke of his cock was meant to drive him insane. It was enough to make him achingly hard but not enough to get him close. He wanted to grab her hand and apply the pressure he desperately craved, but he was also enjoying the gradual build. Besides, two could play at that game.

He moved his fingers inside her and swirled his thumb over her clit so gently, so slowly, she was practically writhing against his hand. He opened his eyes long enough to watch her pull on his cock as she straddled herself on his thighs. "Feels so good," she breathed.

"Mm-hmm... This what you want?"

Her answer was a soft moan and a nod of her head. "So good," she said. "So close."

That was what Wild wanted to hear—that what he was doing to her drove her crazy, made her want to let go. He thought back to the times he'd touched himself while he imagined Jasmine's nude body, all smooth and soft and needy. But the reality of it was so much better than the images his mind could conjure up. Her nipples were hard, her breasts perky and perfectly sized for his hand. He could file away endless fantasies of Jasmine moving over him, her body grinding on his hand with a rhythm that was so sensual and delicate just the mere thought of it would have him hardening in his pants.

When Jasmine's hand sped up and her grip tightened, he nearly let go. And he could tell she was close too by the flush of her chest and the subtle tightening of her pussy, which was so fucking wet, he would drink it up if she'd let him. And he hoped like hell that one day she would, because simply the idea of tasting her—all creamy and warm—had him coming all over his stomach, his abs clenching as his orgasm shot out of him long and hard. A few moments later, she was there with him, melting over his hand as she shook with pleasure, her eyes pressing shut as she bent over him, breathing heavily until she collapsed on his chest.

It was one of the most beautiful things he'd ever seen, and he never wanted to look anywhere else.

CHAPTER SEVENTEEN

Jaz was chatting with a regular when her men arrived at the gym. It was a weird yet pleasant thought: her men. Even though they still hadn't told anyone about their relationships—a fact she was trying not to let bother her; it had only been a few weeks, after all—there was no denying that was exactly what it was in both cases. And it was wonderful and exhilarating while still being challenging and eye-opening. But they'd managed to face the challenges head-on, allowing their bond to grow. She hadn't had sex with either of them yet, but things were definitely heading in that direction on both fronts. It surprised her that neither man seemed particularly bothered by the fact that she would be intimate with both of them, but she wasn't going to ruin it by mentioning it out loud.

She tracked them both as they checked in at the front desk before going their separate ways. Chaz continued to talk, so she assumed she was doing a fairly good job of not letting her disinterest show. Chaz was a nice guy, fit with a handsome face, and he always chatted Jaz up when he saw her. His interest was evident, but she was careful to be friendly without ever flirting back. After a couple more minutes, she excused herself and headed to the office where she'd seen Maddox go.

Leaning up against the doorframe, she watched him

bustle around the office for a minute before he noticed her.

"Hey," he said with a warm smile.

"Hey yourself. Whatcha doing?"

"I misplaced a form I need to send in to our accountant." He resumed his search, shuffling papers around on his desk.

"Did you look on Wild's desk?" she asked as she walked all the way into the room, moving toward the mess that was Wild's workspace.

Maddox looked at it warily. "I'm looking everywhere else before tackling that disaster."

Jaz giggled as she began leafing through papers on Wild's desk. Not that she even knew what she was looking for, but she felt the need to at least *appear* helpful. "We still on for *The Avengers* tonight?"

"Hell yeah. I've been looking forward to seeing it for months."

"Good. And yeah, me too. I love comic book movies."

"Comic book movies?" a voice that Jaz knew was Wild's without turning around asked from behind them. "Oh man, are you guys seeing *Avengers* tonight?" Jaz turned to look at Wild, not missing the look of disappointment that flitted across his face before he chased it away.

"Yeah," Mad said. "Hey, have you seen the form for Jack?"

"Um...maybe? What does it look like?" He walked into the office and settled in next to Jaz to look through the things strewn across his desk.

As Mad described what Wild should look for, Jaz studied the two of them. Despite things developing nicely between them, the three of them hadn't spent much time together. Or any time together really. It was like each man had moved her into a box that didn't involve the other, which was weird as hell considering she *was* involved with the other one. She'd hoped that their resolve to keep things separate would gradually fade and they could go back to all hanging out again. Not that she expected them to be intimate together, but they could all hang out and do stuff together. Couldn't they?

"Found it!" Maddox yelled.

Wild instantly dropped the stack of papers he'd been holding, causing them to plop back onto his desk in even more disarray than they'd been before. Jaz shook her head at him, to which Wild replied with a smirk and a wink.

"You're only in until one, right?" Mad asked her.

"Yeah, I leave right after my noon class."

"Okay, I'm here until six. Is it okay if I pick you up around seven?"

"Why don't I just meet you at your place? That way you don't have to rush."

"You sure you don't mind?" he asked her.

"Nope."

"Okay, then. I'll see you tonight."

"That you will. Later, boys." She waved at them coyly before skipping out of the office to set up for her class.

♦ ♦ ♦ ♦

Maddox and Wild got home a little later than usual, so Mad immediately jumped into the shower. He was looking forward to hanging out with Jaz, just as he always was, but there was also a thrum of unease that was running through him. As he hurried through getting ready, he tried to pinpoint what it was that had him feeling so off, but his brain was half preoccupied with looking good for his date, so the answer remained just out of his mental grasp. He heard the bell ring and rushed to finish dressing, knowing Wild would answer the door. That thought made the cause of his discomfort flash into his mind, but it was gone before he could decipher it.

He walked into the living room, smoothing his hands down his black T-shirt before making sure his wallet was in his pocket. When he looked up, he saw Jaz and Wild on the couch laughing about something. They hadn't noticed him, so he stood there and watched them for a moment. Truth was, as much as he'd liked getting to know Jaz, he missed the three of them hanging out. He knew it was his rule, but now he was wondering if he was maybe ready to get the fuck over it already. But the prospect was still weird to him on some level. Jesus, his life was confusing.

"Wow, you look good." His attention shot to Jaz as she ran appreciative eyes over the T-shirt that barely stretched around his biceps and jeans that hugged his thighs in a way women always seemed to like.

Mad's eyes slid to Wild to gauge his reaction to her perusal, but he was simply smirking as he looked back and forth between them. Looking back at Jaz, Mad said, "You always look good."

She rolled her eyes, but her cheeks pinked a little and her smile was fond. "Ready, sweet talker?"

"Yup." He moved toward the table where he'd thrown his keys when he'd rushed in.

Jaz stood and walked past him, and Wild came into focus behind her. His shoulders looked a little hunched. He grabbed the remote and began clicking through channels. "Have fun," he said, but everything about the scene rubbed Mad wrong. It reminded Mad of all the times Wild was worked up about something but trying his damnedest not to show it.

Mad's unease ramped up, and it became clear what the reason was. Mad and Wild always saw the Marvel movies—and sometimes the DC ones—together. This was the first one since they met that Mad would be seeing without him, and it made Mad's stomach feel like it was dropping a little. But what the hell was he supposed to do? He'd already asked Jaz to the movie. He didn't want to be an asshole by asking her to do something else as they were on their way to the theater.

Mad moved toward the door to join Jaz. "I'll see ya later," he said to Wild.

"Later, guys."

Maddox pulled open the door and then motioned to Jaz to go out first, which she did. Moving behind her, he settled his hand on the doorknob and began to pull it shut, but he stopped before the door was even halfway closed. "This is fucking stupid."

Jaz spun around to look at him. Mad held her gaze for a second before flitting his eyes in Wild's direction. A smile slowly spread across her face, as if she knew where his thoughts had gone. He took that as encouragement and turned to Wild, pushing the door all the way back open. Wild was looking at him like he was crazy, which was likely accurate.

"We always see these movies together," Mad started. "It's

stupid that you're not coming because I'm hung up on the three of us hanging out together."

"It's cool, Mad. I understand," Wild said.

"But I don't. I *want* you to come. How are we going to dissect the movie if you haven't seen it yet? So just...come with us."

Wild looked skeptical and opened his mouth to reply, but Mad cut him off.

"I'm serious. I want you to come. We all used to have a blast hanging out. There's no reason we can't get back to that."

Wild still looked hesitant. "You sure?"

"Yes. Just hurry the fuck up and get changed."

Wild's face lit up, and he jumped off the couch and sprinted into his room. "I'll be ready in five minutes."

Yeah right, Mad thought as he motioned to Jaz to sit back on the couch. Even though he knew Wild had already showered, the man was a prima donna. No way would he be ready in five minutes.

"I'm glad you invited him," Jaz said quietly.

Mad cast a glance toward the hall Wild had just run down. Maybe he would be lucky enough to have the best of both worlds. Maybe it wouldn't explode in his face.

Maybe wasn't usually enough of an assurance for Mad. But in this case...it was.

Looking back at Jaz, he said, "I'm glad too," and picked up the remote to find something for them to watch while they waited for Wild.

♦♦♦♦

Wild had been surprised by Mad's invitation and even more surprised when they fell back into the easy companionship they'd shared before everything had gotten complicated. The movie had been almost as good as the company, and Wild had enjoyed the hell out of the evening. They'd stopped for dinner afterward, and he didn't even tease anyone about their order—mostly because they'd all chosen fairly healthy options, but still. He could always find *something* to give them a hard time about.

When Mad drove back to their place to drop off Wild, Mad and Jaz surprised him by coming inside. He figured they'd escape to have some alone time. When they walked in, Jaz and Mad made themselves comfortable on the couch, and Wild felt the first tingles of awkwardness seep into him. So he reacted in the only way he knew. "So I guess this is the part where I make myself scarce so you two can"—he made his eyebrows jump twice—"get more comfortable. Unless, of course, you'd prefer it if I watched," he said, laughing at his own joke.

When neither of them laughed, Wild silenced immediately.

Jaz tilted her head thoughtfully. "Do you want to watch?"

Wild felt his jaw fall open as he scrambled for something to say. They promised to be honest, but he sure as fuck couldn't tell the truth about this. Could he?

When Wild didn't answer, she looked at Mad. "Do you want Wild to watch?"

Mad locked eyes with her for a second before shifting his

gaze to Wild. The two of them stared at one another for a long moment. Mad seemed to be studying him and clearly came to a decision because he replied while never breaking eye contact with Wild, "Yeah. I do." His voice was gruff and sincere.

What the fuck did Wild do now?

"So?" Jaz's question startled him because he'd still been looking at Mad, trying to figure out if the guy actually meant what he'd said. There was no indication that he'd been lying, which gave Wild the push he needed to say what he was thinking.

"Fuck yeah, I wanna watch," he said quickly, his voice raspy.

Both Jaz and Mad laughed at his reply.

There were so many ways this could go wrong. Would Mad freak out afterward? Wild was pretty sure Mad understood that this wasn't really about watching Mad. It was about watching someone he trusted taking Jaz apart in the hottest possible ways. But when Wild thought about it, since Mad was the only one he trusted that much, he guessed it kind of was about Mad in that sense. Wild could count on Mad to take care of someone Wild felt possessive over. To give her pleasure while Wild took a seat and enjoyed the show.

Jaz refocused on Mad and leaned toward him, capturing his lips in a kiss that was gentle at first but quickly ramped up in intensity. Mad shoved his hands in Jaz's hair and tilted her head so he could kiss her more soundly. Jaz moved so she was straddling him and began gyrating on him in a way that made Mad break the kiss and groan. Jaz used the break to kiss down Mad's neck, her hands roving down his chest and stomach until she reached the hem of his shirt. She pulled it up, and Mad lifted his arms so she could remove it.

He did the same to her white off-the-shoulder top and threw it behind him. She rocked against him harder, and his hands went to her ass, pulling her roughly into him.

Wild's dick was like an iron bar in his jeans. He wasn't sure watching was such a good idea anymore, since he was pretty sure he'd either come in his pants like a teenager or need to run out of the room and attend to his aching cock. He hadn't given much thought to how he'd feel actually *watching* Jaz with someone else, but it didn't bother him at all. Which probably had a lot to do with the fact that the other person was Mad, whom Wild trusted with his life. Wild could trust him with this too.

Jaz stood just long enough for them both to remove their pants, and then she climbed back into Mad's lap. Mad's hands swept over her skin roughly until they rested on her back and worked to unclasp her white strapless bra. The small piece of material fell away, revealing Jaz's pert breasts that were just big enough to get a handful of—which Wild knew from experience.

She reached her hand down between them and slipped it into Mad's boxers, and Wild could tell she was stroking him as Mad sucked on her nipples. The two of them were all unrestrained passion, and if Wild hadn't known for a fact they hadn't fucked yet, he'd have thought they'd been long-term lovers. They toyed with one another's bodies as if they knew them almost as well as they knew their own. Knowing they'd fooled around accounted for some of it, but it didn't completely explain the harmony that seemed to exist between them. It was enthralling to watch, and Wild felt like the luckiest son of a bitch on the planet to get to witness it.

Mad whispered something in Jaz's ear before he sucked on the lobe. When he let go, Jaz leaned back as Mad grabbed her hips. She fell almost all the way back until she could reach his jeans on the floor. Riffling through them, she pulled out his wallet and retrieved a condom. Then she pulled herself back up, tearing open the condom wrapper and rising up on her knees just enough to give Mad room to push his boxers down. Gravity took care of the rest, and the garment fell to the floor.

Jaz rolled the latex down his hard cock, both of them staring intently as her hand moved down the length of him. Wild imagined what it would feel like to have Jaz smooth a condom down his own erection—to know that any second he'd be able to plunge into her with an unrestrained passion he hadn't experienced with her before. It made him both excited for Mad and envious at the same time.

When she was done, Mad pulled the fabric of her white thong to the side, and Jaz lined herself up with him and then slowly sank down onto him until she was fully seated. Her hands gripped the back of the couch as her head tilted back, a deep moan coming from her throat. They stayed still for a moment, maybe giving Jaz a second to adjust, before she raised herself up a bit so she could lower herself down all over again.

As their pace picked up, Wild palmed himself through his jeans. He'd tried to hold off for as long as he could, not wanting to make any of this about him. But watching Maddox make her move like that, moan like that, made him unable to leave his own dick out of the equation. Part of him was desperate to pull his cock out so he could stroke it as he watched, but a bigger part of him kept him from doing it. This was about Mad and Jaz, and while they'd invited him to watch, they hadn't invited him to participate. Wild felt like jerking his cock would make this moment about him, when that wasn't at all what it was. It was about all of them on some level, but it was principally about Mad and Jaz connecting in a way they'd yet to do before that moment. The fact that Wild had been granted permission to stay seemed appropriate, though. This relationship had been something all three of them had discovered together. It felt right that they were all present when it progressed to something profoundly more intimate.

Mad began lifting his hips, thrusting up into Jaz as she slammed down on him. The sound of their bodies meeting filled the room, and it was like an erotic soundtrack that made Wild's dick jerk in his pants like the fucker had rhythm.

"Oh God, oh God," Jaz began chanting as Mad's face began to show signs of strain.

Wild recognized the faces of two people who were close to climaxing. It was hot as fuck. And Wild knew as soon as they were done, he was going to have to attend to his own erection, because there was no fucking way that was going away on its own.

"Christ, you feel so fucking good," Mad grunted.

"Right there, Mad. Don't stop."

Wild let his hand rub the hard outline in his pants as he begged them to both hurry the fuck up so he could go jerk off and keep going so the sweet torture could continue.

Mad began to grunt, each thrust into Jaz making the sound louder and grittier. Jaz was practically keening. Suddenly, Jaz's body seemed to lock up, her muscles going rigid before she began to shake with her orgasm. She threw herself forward, draping herself over Mad, who continued fucking up into her. Her body continued to convulse, and Wild could only imagine how that felt around Mad's cock—her entire pussy slick and tightening around him. Wild couldn't fucking wait to experience it for himself.

Jaz seemed to come back to herself just in time for Mad to lose it. She sat up straighter and ground down on him as he thrust for the final time, shuddering as he clearly climaxed. Wild felt a ripple of envy go through him that Mad got off while Wild felt like even the softest touch would make him explode.

Mad's eyes were squeezed shut, and he scraped his hands down her back as he rode out his release. He gave a few more shallow pumps before his body began to relax. When he opened his eyes, he smiled up at Jaz, which she returned before leaning down to kiss him.

This seemed more intimate than the fucking, and Wild was just about to get up to give them their privacy when Mad said, "I'm going to go clean up. Maybe you can use that time to take care of your boy."

Was he saying what Wild thought he was saying?

Jaz looked over at Wild, her eyes bright and a smirk on her face. "I think I can handle that." She slid off Mad's lap and dropped to her knees. Maddox stood quickly and made his way toward the hallway without saying another word.

Jaz crawled toward Wild, the intent in her eyes clear.

When she reached Wild, she pushed his knees all the way apart so she could fit between them. Maintaining eye contact with him, she moved her hands to his jeans and undid his belt and popped the button free. As her fingers began pulling down his zipper, he reached out and grasped her wrists. Her eyes darted to his.

"You sure?" he asked.

"Fuck yeah," she replied, stealing his words from earlier.

Wild stared at her for a second, looking for any hesitance in her expression, but he saw none. He tugged on her wrists, pulling her to him so he could give her a quick but hard kiss before releasing her and settling back in the recliner.

Jaz pulled the zipper down and prompted Wild to lift his hips just enough so she could pull his jeans and briefs down. Wasting no time, Jaz wrapped her hand around his shaft and jerked it slowly, her fist tight and perfect around him. It wasn't the first time she'd had her hand on his dick, but it was the first time he was on a hair trigger. She rubbed her thumb over his slit, sliding his pre-come all around the head before she dipped her head and took his cock into her mouth.

Wild let his head fall back and his eyes fall closed as she bobbed up and down on him. A groan made its way up from low in his throat at the wet heat surrounding his cock. He opened his eyes again because he wanted to watch her. He tangled his hand in her hair and held it back from her face as she hollowed her cheeks and took him deep.

"Jesus fuck. Not gonna last long," he warned her.

She hummed around him, and the vibrations nearly made him lose it. Pulling off for a second, she licked at his head as she cupped his balls and rolled them gently. Her gaze stayed on him as she tongued his slit before she went down on him again. He couldn't resist bucking his hips slightly as his orgasm bore down in him.

His spine tingled as pleasure raced down it before it seemed to explode in his groin. He tried to pull Jaz off just as he was about to come, but she refused to budge, and he couldn't hold off for another fucking second. His need to let go took hold of him, consumed all of him, until his cock was jerking with every burst of his release. Jaz swallowed his come greedily. When she licked the tip of his cock, making sure she got every drop, Wild's body spasmed again as if he were dry-coming.

She looked up, and Wild couldn't resist. He leaned forward and captured her mouth with his. He knew some guys didn't like the taste of themselves on someone's tongue, but Wild reveled in it.

When they finally pulled away from one another, Jaz looked at him. "Well, this night took an unexpected turn."

Wild laughed like he so often did when Jaz was around.

"That's a good thing, though, right?" He thought he knew the answer but wanted to make sure.

"Fuck yeah," she repeated again, causing them both to laugh before they shared one more lingering kiss.

Fuck yeah was right.

CHAPTER EIGHTEEN

Jaz sat on the couch at Wild and Mad's apartment, nestled against Mad with her feet in Wild's lap. If anyone had told her a few months ago that this would become her life, she'd never have believed them. It had been a whirlwind of dates with her men individually, broken up by what they all simply called "hanging out." It seemed to have been almost an unconscious decision by all three to use different terms to punctuate their expectations.

If Wild told Mad he had a *date* with Jaz, Mad knew to make other plans. But if Wild said they were *hanging out*, Mad would ask what they were doing and plan on joining them. The same went for Wild. It was almost bizarre how well they'd all melded together; Jaz had certainly expected more growing pains than they'd had. Maybe it was still the honeymoon phase—likely—or maybe it was because there was always a third person to step in and mediate before anything got blown out of proportion—also likely.

And as Jaz hung out with both guys, everyone comfortable and relaxed, she was thankful she got to have this. Pressed up against Mad, Jaz's mind wandered to their date last week. Or more specifically to *after* the date, when she'd really gotten to see what all his hard muscles could do.

They'd been at work, which had always been a strict subtle-flirting-no-touching area. And while Wild held to the same professional standard, Mad was more of a stickler about being discreet at the gym. Something Jaz completely understood and respected—until Mad broke his own rule. The memory made her smile—and squirm a bit.

Jaz had been tasked with closing the gym with Mad, and out of sheer boredom while he did whatever it was he did in his office, she had gone into the supply closet in one of their multipurpose rooms to organize the equipment. It was almost ten p.m., and she still had an hour to kill. As she sorted bands by color and resistance, she wondered if she could possibly bribe the guys to never make her close ever again.

"There you are," a familiar voice said from behind her.

She smiled but didn't turn around as Mad approached. When he wrapped his hands around her hips from behind, she startled slightly, not expecting Mad to be so demonstrative at work, even though they were fairly hidden.

His lips went to her neck, kissing and sucking a line down to her collarbone. Then he moved closer to her, allowing her to feel his hard length pressing into her back.

"This is your fault," he said gruffly. "The entire time I was training clients, I kept getting glimpses of you. By the time my last one ended, I was rock fucking hard, and I had to hide in my office. But the fucker won't go away. Need you."

Jaz's body flushed with heat at his words. Mad, the man who never lost control, was confessing his need for her, and damned if she didn't reciprocate the feelings. "Take me," she whispered.

His hands drifted into the waistband of her compression pants, past the fabric of her thong, until finally reaching her clit. He pushed his erection against her ass as he fingered her.

Letting her head drop back against his solid chest, she gave herself over to the sensations this man was causing. A soft moan left her lips as he swirled his finger around her clit, stroking her perfectly. Then his fingers abruptly left her.

He began pushing at her pants as he said, "Take these off." The words came out like an order, and Jaz quickly complied, kicking off her sneakers and sweeping her pants and thong off her body.

She turned to look at him as he pushed his shorts down enough to free his hard shaft. Unable to resist, she gripped his cock in her hand and gave it a few strokes. He watched her hand move avidly for a moment before he tore open a condom he must have brought in with him. "Pretty confident you were going to get lucky, huh?" she murmured.

He shot her a cocky grin as he rolled the latex onto his length. Then he reached for her, cupping her ass and hoisting her up.

Jaz wrapped her legs around him instinctively as he moved them so her back was against the wall. He didn't slam her against it, but he wasn't gentle either. It was...perfect. Being manhandled by a man who'd never actually hurt her ratcheted up her lust even more.

Mad wasted no time before pushing into her, grunting as his hard cock slid into her body. "Fuck," he breathed out as he bottomed out inside her.

"Yeah. Let's keep doing that."

Mad laughed at her reply, but it only lasted a second. Growing serious again, he thrust into her, using the power from his thick thighs and sculpted ass. The man had better never stop doing squats if being able to fuck her like this was the result.

Jaz's back grazed along the wall, the rough surface the perfect accompaniment to the beautiful roughness of Mad taking her with a kind of uncontrolled abandon she hadn't experienced from him before. She did her best to grind down on him every time he pumped into her, but they were both so lost to pleasure it was difficult to retain any sense of coordination.

Their pants and moans filled the room, along with words gritted out in the heat of their passion. "More," "Fuck," "Harder," and "Yes" filtered through the air, though Jaz could barely process who was saying what. Fucking Mad in that moment was as close to an out-of-body experience as Jaz had ever had.

Mad began bucking into her even harder, but whatever finesse he had was gone. This was the homestretch for both of them, and they were giving it all they had without concern for it being pretty. Jaz clutched him, positioning herself so her clit made contact with his pelvis on each pass. "So close," she moaned.

She screwed her eyes shut and focused on the feeling of Mad owning her body. Though her eyes were closed, she envisioned what his cock looked like as it moved in and out of her. The erotic image she conjured made fireworks ignite behind her eyelids as her spine arched and seemed to lock in place while her orgasm barreled down on her.

Her body shook in Mad's tight hold as he pumped into her one...two...three more times before pushing deep and holding himself there, his cock clearly emptying his release. Mad gave a couple more soft thrusts before he stilled, his hands moving to her back as they embraced and came down from their orgasms. He didn't move to put her down, and she was thankful though not surprised.

She was hopeful Mad would never let her go.

Wild idly rubbed Jaz's feet as they watched the movie. Normally, Wild would lose himself in it, but tonight his attention kept straying to the woman who wriggled her toes in his lap every time he stopped rubbing them. He smirked and gave her calf a pinch, making her jerk slightly and giggle before he resumed his light massage. His hands began to ghost up her feet to her lower leg, causing her skin to break out in goose bumps. It wasn't the first time he'd caused such a reaction in her. The thought made him have to bite back a groan as he thought back to the night of the benefit.

"What time do we have to be there?" Jaz had called from her bathroom, where she'd been rushing to finish getting ready.

"Reservation's in ten minutes."

"Shit," he'd heard her mutter as he stopped in the doorway of her bathroom. He took in her reflection in the mirror as she applied eyeliner. Wild had scored two tickets to a benefit one of his clients was hosting on behalf of a community center for underprivileged youth in their area, and Wild had jumped at the chance to go. He didn't typically have much of an excuse to get dressed up but had fun doing so from time to time. Jaz had seemed to share his enthusiasm.

"I don't know how I got so behind," she explained as she dug around in her makeup bag.

"Takes time to look that good," he said, meaning every word. She was wearing a red dress that cupped her breasts perfectly and showed off her trim figure. It managed to not leave a whole lot to the imagination yet still be classy, which turned him on to no end.

"You don't look so bad yourself," she said with a smile Wild could only classify as seductive.

Wild looked down at himself—at his charcoal-gray trousers with a matching vest that he wore over a blue button-down. He knew he'd sweat to death if he wore a jacket and felt like the vest added enough sophistication to justify skipping it. "Yeah? You like what you see?"

"I always like what I see," she replied as she added mascara to her long lashes. Once she'd put the cap back on it and dropped it into her bag, Wild moved up behind her.

Sliding his hands around her hips, he rested his chin on her shoulder. "I always like what I see too."

Her hands came to rest on top of his as she gave him a dazzling smile. Wild turned his head so he could press a kiss to her neck. But Wild wasn't able to leave it at one and began trailing kisses down to her exposed shoulder.

Tilting her head to give him more access, she warned, "If you start this, we're never going to make it."

"We're going to be late regardless. Might as well make it worth it." He grabbed her hips and spun her around, making her shriek before laughing. He smiled with her as he pressed her back into her sink. But both of their faces grew serious as his hands drifted up her thighs, lifting the hem of her dress as they went. Wild felt her skin pebbling as his fingers lightly roved over the soft flesh there.

Her breathing picked up when he moved his hands higher, trailing over her inner thighs but diverting course as they approached where she likely wanted his touch the most. He pulled her dress up so that it gathered around her stomach and he was free to roam his fingertips over her pelvis. She wore a red satin thong, and he liked seeing his fingers tease against the material.

"Please, Wild," she whispered.

Unable to hold off any longer, he gripped her thong and pushed it down her legs. Then he let his fingers make contact with her clit. Feeling how wet she already was turned him on even more. He watched her chest rise and fall as her hands gripped the edge of the sink. When she threw her head back and moaned, Wild lost all restraint.

He pulled his wallet out of his back pocket and withdrew a condom. Then he quickly undid his pants and pushed them and his briefs down, letting his rigid cock spring free.

"Hurry," she ordered, and Wild heeded her words.

Rolling the latex down his cock, he positioned himself at her entrance and pushed inside in one smooth thrust. She wrapped her hands around his neck as he lifted her so that her ass was atop the sink, putting her at the perfect height for him to fuck her.

He moved in and out of her with a speed and power that

definitely earned him his name. Everything about them both was wild in that moment: the way they clung desperately to one another, the way their bodies joined loudly with every pump of his hips, the way their moans and groans filled the room.

Their sex always seemed to be this way: needy and consuming. Even when they started sweet and slow, it never remained that way. It was as if their passion for one another burned too hot to contain.

Wild felt his orgasm building as his cock slid against the slick walls of her pussy. "Play with yourself," he told her, needing her to go over the edge with him.

She somehow got one hand between them, and he felt her fingers moving as she toyed with her clit. Her breaths came in pants, letting him know she was close too.

"That's it," he whispered. "Wanna feel you come on my dick."

"Oh, oh, ooooh fuck," she moaned as her body shook with her climax. She leaned into him as aftershocks shot through her.

He felt her fingers drift back, touching where he pumped into her. That, coupled with the way her pussy contracted around him, and he was done for, following her over the crest of their release. He thrust into her one final time as he filled the condom.

Jaz buried her face in his neck and continued to cling to him, which was just fine with Wild. Having a woman like this leaning on him filled him with so many good feelings, his post-sex brain couldn't even identify them all. So he wrapped his arms firmly around her and let himself simply bask in it.

♦ ♦ ♦ ♦

Mad wasn't sure how long they'd been watching the movie Wild had picked, but he wasn't into it. He'd never been a fan of science fiction, so the second he'd seen the word "space" in the description, he'd begun to protest. But when he realized Jaz seemed interested, he'd quickly acquiesced. Not only was he much more inclined to make concessions for her than he was for Wild, but he also knew when he was outnumbered. And there was no way he'd win against those two, so it wasn't worth trying.

"I thought you promised I'd like this?" he said, reaching down to tickle her side before giving her a kiss on the forehead.

"Did I promise that?" she asked innocently. "I'm pretty sure it was Wild who said that."

"No way," Wild said. "You're not pinning this one on me." Then he held her foot so he could tickle it without her getting away, and before Mad knew it, they both had her in hysterics.

"Stop!" she pleaded. "No more. I can't breathe."

They let up for a second, but as Wild pointed out, if she really couldn't breathe, she wouldn't be talking.

"You guys are assholes," she said between laughs.

"Well, that's not going to get you what you want," Mad teased. "Is it, Wild?"

Wilder pretended to think for a moment before saying "Nope" and continuing to tickle her. Jasmine was flailing around, but the guys had a good hold on her, and Mad could tell she had no intention of escaping anyway. "What about this?" Wild asked. "Any better?" He was kissing her lightly on the inside of her foot before working his way up to the inside of her ankle.

Jasmine seemed to squirm a bit, but Mad recognized it as a movement more of pleasure than protest. "Yes. Much," she said.

"How about this?" Maddox asked before dipping down to brush his lips softly against the skin just below her ear. He knew this spot drove her crazy, as did the top of her back—which he went after next—and before long, both men had her practically bucking off the couch as she begged them for more.

"What do you want?" Wild asked, his eyes locking with hers as he held her ankle over his shoulder and kissed her calf. His hand moved up the outside of her thigh and drifted under her high-waisted shorts before dragging them slowly down her legs.

Mad felt like he was watching some sort of porn he was somehow allowed to be a part of, and fuck if he didn't love the hell out of it. His cock was tenting his mesh shorts, and he wanted to jerk himself so fucking badly already as his eyes fixed on the way Wild spread Jasmine's legs so he could gain access to her pussy. Mad remembered how warm she was, how wet she always was when he pressed his fingers inside, and though a part of him wished it were his tongue lapping at her right now, another part he didn't even know existed found it oddly erotic to watch his best friend give her pleasure.

Maddox knew Wild was probably just as turned on as he was, and he couldn't help but wonder how all of this would play out. Who, if either of them, would get to have sex with her? Who would be the one to make her come? Only one other time had the three of them been present during any sexual act. Mad had been the lucky one that night, so it was pretty much a given that Wild had this one. Maddox would have to be content to be the spectator here.

He watched both of them for a few more moments before he couldn't take it any longer. With his free hand, he began to palm himself while he played with Jaz's nipples through her tank top. How the hell hadn't he noticed before now that she wasn't wearing a bra?

He tried so fucking hard to only focus on Jaz—like how wet her mouth was when she brought his fingers into it and sucked them like they were his cock. But every so often, his eyes would wander to what Wild was doing.

Wild had been kissing her stomach but then moved up and knelt between her legs. Jaz reached down and took him in her hand. With his hands behind his head, Wild seemed to give himself over to what Jasmine was doing, his hips moving back and forth so he could thrust into her grip.

And somehow it didn't matter to Maddox that he was looking at his friend's dick, because Jasmine's hand was around it, jacking him with long strokes. It was all so fucking hot, so unexpected.

Maddox did the same to himself over his shorts, letting the fabric graze lightly over his skin until he needed to grip himself harder, pull faster. He groaned but, feeling slightly awkward, tried to stifle it. A few seconds later, Jaz moved to sit up so she could take Wild in her mouth, and the sounds that came from them had Maddox wondering whether he should come in his pants or excuse himself to go finish in the bathroom. Jasmine's head moved back and forth, and her hand swirled over the remaining length of Wild's shaft that she couldn't fit in her mouth.

Wild grabbed her head, played with her hair as she sucked him, and Maddox nearly lost it when he heard the suction of her lips on Wild's cock.

"Fuck him," Maddox said, surprising even himself. He hadn't known how badly he wanted to watch that happen until he'd voiced it. But if watching Jasmine give Wild a blow job had Maddox this fucking hot, he could only imagine what seeing them together would do—focusing on the two of them as they connected in a way that was so intimate Mad couldn't help but feel a part of it even if he wasn't. With Jasmine and Wilder, Maddox didn't feel the need to censor himself or what he wanted. This was about what *felt* right, not what he *thought* was right.

Wild looked at Maddox, his eyes asking if he was serious without actually having to speak the question. And Mad never had to answer because Wild knew him well enough to read the sincerity in his expression. A few moments later, Wild got up to get a condom. He returned to Jasmine and gave her a lingering kiss before rolling it on. Within seconds he was inside her, his hands gripping her hips roughly as he pulled her onto him.

Jasmine wrapped her legs around his waist and moaned with every thrust, her head leaning back as her back arched off the couch. Everything about her was sexy. The way her hair drifted back to cover part of Maddox's shorts and how her fingers played with her own nipples like she knew better than anyone what would make her hotter.

"Will you touch yourself for me?" Maddox asked her.

Her answer was a hand grazing over her torso until it reached her clit. But she didn't move right away. "I'm gonna come soon if I do this."

"I'm right there with you," Maddox assured her. "I wanna see it. *Hear* it."

With that, her fingers moved in small circles over herself. Slowly, gently, she pleasured herself as Maddox did the same to himself and Wild pumped into her, his face straining with an obvious need to come.

"Fuck," Maddox said. "Can't wait." He was pulling on himself hard, seconds away from losing all control.

"Let me taste you," she said, reaching back with her free hand to touch his cock through his shorts.

Maddox nearly jumped up, because if he didn't, he was going to come before his dick could reach Jasmine's mouth, and that was definitely *not* something he wanted to happen. He leaned over her, propping himself up with his hand on the back of the couch. Pulling his shorts down just enough that his cock could spring free, he jerked himself rapidly with his fingertips, watching Jaz below him until she began to come.

It was the sound of her soft curses and heated breaths that had him squeezing himself hard as his release shot onto her. He pumped himself slowly a few more times until he was done, and the feel of her tongue licking the extra from the tip of his cock had him wanting to go for round two. He wasn't sure how much even made it into her mouth, and he didn't really care. The whole thing was so fucking hot. Wild thrust inside her a few more times before he plunged deep and held himself there while he climaxed.

Maddox couldn't quite identify when his life had taken such a sharp turn that he could be turned on watching his friend sleep with the girl he liked, maybe even loved, but that seemed to be his current situation.

And though it was admittedly weird as hell, he didn't want it any other way.

CHAPTER NINETEEN

Before grabbing a spatula from the metal container next to the stove, Jasmine waved her hand over the smoke coming from the pan and turned on the stove exhaust fan.

"First time cooking?" Wild said, sliding his arms around her waist and sniffing her neck rapidly like he was a puppy. He knew it made her squirm, and she swatted him with the spatula. "Ouch," he said. "That stung."

"Good," she said after flipping the burgers. She turned around to face him and then hopped up on their countertop so Wild could position himself between her legs.

"When did Mad say he's getting home?"

She couldn't help but laugh. "Since when does kissing my neck make you think of Maddox?"

Wilder laughed too—one of his deep raucous chuckles that meant he really thought something was funny. "Since you smell like burned bacon and cheeseburgers. I'm hungry, but we told Mad we'd wait for him."

She looked at the microwave clock. "He's actually later than he said he'd be. I'm surprised he's not home yet."

Wilder continued making a path from her neck down to nip along her collarbone. "Guess we'll have to occupy ourselves for a few more minutes then."

"Guess so," she said, her head drifting back to give him more access. It crossed her mind to let him have her right here in their kitchen, but she'd already managed to burn their meal, and she didn't want to risk burning *them* too.

A few minutes later, they heard Mad open the door and toss his keys on the table next to it. "Hey," he called. "What'd you guys burn?"

Wild laughed again right as Jaz yelled, "You guys are relentless."

Mad appeared in the kitchen and walked over to give her a kiss. "You teased her about it too, I guess?" he asked Wild, who nodded and muttered, "Of course."

Grabbing three beers from the fridge, Mad said, "Sorry I'm late. I got stuck talking to Kat from 3C. She's...something," he said with a shake of his head.

"She hit on you too?" Jasmine asked with a laugh.

"Yeah. Like out of nowhere. I hadn't even met her until tonight." After opening the beers, he handed Wild and Jaz the others. "Wait...Kat hit on *you*?" he asked Jaz.

"No," she said with a loud laugh. "She hit on Wild one day when she was dropping off your mail, and I overheard her."

Mad raised an eyebrow. "Well, you'll have to let her know your men are taken."

She jumped down from the counter and slid the burgers onto plates.

"Helps if you turn the burner off too," Wild said with a wink.

Jasmine would've liked to think that she had no idea why her mind seemed to be elsewhere tonight, but it would've been a lie. She'd been waiting until both of them were home so she could tell them the news. And she hoped they were just as excited to hear it as she was. "Speaking of 'my men,'" she said, "I want to ask you guys something."

Mad and Wild exchanged curious glances that also seemed to hold more than a hint of anxiety.

"It's good, I swear," she said. "You know how my mom's getting married in a few weeks, right?" She didn't give them time to respond before saying, "Well, it took some convincing, but I finally wore her down and she agreed to let me have a plus two."

Mad had been about to take a sip of his beer, but the bottle hovered just below his lips like her comment had caused his entire body to cease working altogether. His mouth was slightly open, but he hadn't said anything yet, and as far as she could tell, he hadn't even blinked since she'd spoken.

She looked to Wild, hoping to get a better reaction, but the only thing he said was, "I don't really do parents." Then he took a sip of his beer like his words hadn't just punched her in the face.

Finally, Maddox found his voice. "Jasmine, you know I'd love to go. But...we...*we*," he said, emphasizing that he was referring to the three of them, "can't go to a wedding together." The two men were so different from one another, but somehow they managed to find a way to be assholes at the same time.

"Why?" It was a simple question, but she knew Mad would have trouble answering it.

"I don't know," Mad said, sounding oddly squeamish. "It's just...weird, that's all."

"Weird to who? You?"

"Everyone. How do you explain to people that you got to bring two dates?"

"Seriously, Maddox? That's what you're worried about? Other people thinking it's unfair? Come on."

"Um...just so we're clear, *I'm* not going to *any* wedding," Wild said. "So you can just take Mad if you want. Problem solved."

She glared at him, wishing she could slap the casual expression off his face. "The problem *isn't* solved. Because the wedding isn't the fucking problem. The problem is the two of you."

"Us?" they both said in unison.

"Yeah, you. I thought we had a good thing here. We've been together for months. *Together*," she said again. "As in the three of us. Jesus, Maddox. I thought by now you might be able to accept that this relationship isn't a conventional one."

"You think I don't realize that?"

"Oh, I know you realize that, but I'm talking about acceptance. And accepting it means that you have to be okay with other people knowing about it eventually."

"Yeah, eventually," Mad said. "I thought we agreed to take this at a pace we're comfortable with?"

"We did," she said, conceding him that. She was quiet for a few moments before saying, "I guess I'm just worried that eventually will never come. That this'll be all it ever is between all of us—hanging out in public and dating in private." She'd been looking at the floor, running her toe over the grout in the tile, but she looked up at the men, who somehow had the nerve to stare at her like she was the crazy one. "I need more than this," she said. "Maybe I didn't realize it until now, but I need more. What we have is special. It's not something to be embarrassed of."

"Again," Wilder said, "I'm not embarrassed. I just don't want to meet anyone's family. I'm not really the take-home kind of guy."

"I heard you the first time," she said, her voice intentionally cold. "And don't worry, Wild Man," she mocked. "Right now, I wouldn't even take you to the hospital if you had a gunshot wound, let alone to an event as important as my mother's wedding. I seriously can't believe you guys."

She shook her head, hoping the gesture would convey her disgust with their responses, but they were so fucking dense sometimes, she had no idea if it would. "I can't believe I thought you'd be excited that you could both go." She felt tears start to sting behind her eyes, but she refused to let them fall. Not while these two cowards could see them anyway. Walking toward their door, she didn't even bother to look over her shoulder. "At least I was right about one thing. You two are perfect for each other."

"What's that supposed to mean?" Wild called.

"Jaz, wait," Maddox called, his voice pleading.

But she didn't. She opened the door and let it shut behind her without saying another word. She was done waiting.

CHAPTER TWENTY

Wild returned a pair of dumbbells that had been left out, dropping them into their spots on the metal rack loudly. "What do these people think? We're fucking maids?" he muttered to himself, though the raised eyebrows of one of the members nearby told Wild he hadn't been as quiet as he'd thought. Holding the guy's stare, Wild felt a hint of satisfaction when the other guy looked away first, though it was short-lived.

Sighing, Wild made his way back toward the front of the gym, silently chastising himself for losing his cool. Something he'd been doing a lot lately. But he hadn't punched anything yet, so it could be worse. Because that was what Wild wanted to do. He wanted to hit something. Smash it to bits with his bare hands until it lay crumbled at his feet—a jumbled mass that used to be whole but now couldn't be repaired.

The image was almost poetic in its symbolism.

As Wild approached the front desk, he noticed Jaz was sitting there talking with Yohanna, so he veered off and made his way to the office. It didn't escape his notice that he was being a fucking coward, but he didn't particularly care either. This was why Wild hated doing long-term relationships. The fallout was always messy as fuck—confrontational and depressing. And while Wild would go toe-to-toe with anyone if the need arose, emotional confrontations were a whole other animal. An animal Wild avoided as if it were a rabid raccoon.

He hurried into the office, stopping short when he saw Mad inside. He took a deep breath and made his way to his desk and sat down. It wasn't that he and Mad were avoiding one another exactly—they lived together, for Christ's sake—but they'd definitely been giving each other space. And it was weird and awkward, and Wild hated it but didn't know how to bridge the Jaz-sized gap between them. He began shuffling papers around on his desk in an attempt to look like he had a purpose for being there, when a knock on the door sounded behind him.

Slightly startled, Wild spun his chair around quickly and caught sight of Jaz standing in the doorway. He glanced over at Mad, seeing that he was likewise looking at Jaz, papers hanging in his hands as he stared.

"Can I come in?" she asked, and the two of them nodded like morons. Jaz stepped farther into the room but didn't move to close the door.

It was the first time the three of them had been alone, and the air was thick with tension. Wild felt as if his skin was vibrating, like a wild bird that lived in his veins was trying to escape this awkward-as-fuck situation by pecking holes in his skin.

"What's up?" Mad asked, his voice gravelly. He coughed to clear his throat but didn't say anything more.

Wild saw Jaz's chest rise and fall with a deep breath before she spoke. "I was going to head home a few days earlier than initially planned. Thought my mom might appreciate the help."

Thoughts raged through Wild's head. Thoughts about all of the unspoken things she could be saying. She'd called it *home*. Wasn't this her home? Was she going back early to look for a new job? Would she decide not to come back? Could this really be it? The last time he saw her? Words like *stay, please, fix, chance, try, better, please, stay* whirled through his brain so quickly he was dizzy with them. They wanted to shoot out of his mouth, each one needing only a voice to become a truth that would settle him. But each one died in his throat before they could ever be uttered.

Instead, "You'll let us know, right? If you're not planning on returning?" were the words he went with, and as soon as they were out, Wild knew every one of them was wrong. Each of them only served to further crack what was already broken. He saw it in the tic in her jaw, the narrowing if her eyes, the set of her shoulders.

"Why wouldn't I return?" she asked, her voice cold and so un-Jaz-like, Wild felt the loss of her dig deeper into his marrow.

Wild shrugged. Shrugged like he had no stake in this game. Was he becoming a pod person? It was as if the connection between the physical and metaphysical had frayed, leaving him appearing callous and aloof when inside he felt like a fucking Nicholas Sparks movie.

"Just in case an opportunity presented itself when you were back home," Maddox supplied, saving Wild from becoming an even bigger dick. "We'd just like to know. We wouldn't blame you or anything."

Jaz snorted. "How kind of you."

"I didn't mean... I just... We... We'd understand—"

Mad was faltering, and it was Wild's turn to play hero. "We'd understand if being here has lost its appeal," he said softly.

Jaz crossed her arms over her chest. "Is this a roundabout way of telling me it would be best if I found a new job?"

She tried her best to mask it, but Wild, who'd spent months memorizing everything about her, saw the vulnerability in the question. It made him want to rip the cause of it apart—even though he was the cause.

"No. We are definitely not telling you that," Mad said, his voice firm.

She looked over at Wild then, clearly waiting for him to speak as well.

The words echoed through his mind again. S*tay, please, fix, chance, try, better, please, stay.* But again, he didn't speak them. "If you think I want to teach yoga, you're nuts."

She let her arms drop back to her sides, her posture slackening. Wild allowed himself the spark of pleasure he felt at putting her at ease.

"Then I'll be back. Tuesday morning, like we discussed."

"Sounds good," Mad said with a smile that didn't reach his eyes.

"Have a good time," Wild added.

Jaz gave them a nod and a small smile that looked more sad than anything else. Then she turned and left the room, leaving the office feeling emptier than Wild had ever experienced.

Both men stared after her a second before turning their gazes on each other. There was so much to be said, so much to confess, so much to share. The moment was heavy with opportunity, the words still there. S*tay, please, fix, chance, try, better, please, stay.*

But instead of voicing anything, both men let the moment pass and turned back to their desks.

CHAPTER TWENTY-ONE

"You almost done?" Wild asked, appearing a few feet from where Maddox was lifting.

"Don't know. Why?" Mad jerked the barbell above his head before letting it drop to his feet. The sound of it hitting the rubber mats gave him a sort of satisfaction he couldn't describe.

"I was gonna head out and figured maybe you'd wanna grab a beer or something."

"What's the occasion?" Mad asked, sliding some more weight onto one side of the barbell. Wild grabbed a weight and took care of the other side. "Thanks."

"Since when does there need to be an occasion for us to grab a beer?"

Mad shrugged before approaching the bar and setting up for his next lift. He brought it up to his chest easily, but getting it over his head proved to be more of a problem. Dropping under the weight didn't help, and he let the bar fall to the ground again, though this time, it was out of frustration. He brought an arm up to his head to wipe away some sweat. "That would've been a PR," he said, aware that he hadn't answered Wilder's question. Though really, Wild should know the answer. Things had been even weirder since Jaz left. Like her absence in the gym caused her absence in their lives to become even more noticeable.

"Try it again," Wild said, leaning down to tighten the weights that had moved a bit with the fall.

"I will," Mad said, sounding more defensive than he meant to. But he wasn't one to give up after trying one time. Wild knew that better than anyone. It was how they were able to keep a successful business going, why their bodies looked like they were flesh on top of granite, how they lived their lives. But there was a time when that hadn't been true for Maddox—a time when he'd been ready to give up without a fight. He couldn't stop the memory from pushing itself to the front of his brain, where it manifested with such vivid clarity he felt like he was reliving it.

"What'd you lose?"

Maddox jerked his head up, startled by a voice when he thought for sure his only company was a bird that had settled on part of a nearby truss. "What?" He turned toward the voice and saw a shaggy-haired blond kid staring back at him. He was skinnier than Maddox but looked to be in pretty good shape. Turning his head farther, Mad saw an old gray sedan parked on the small shoulder of the bridge.

"You drop your phone or something?" the kid asked. And before Maddox could answer, he continued. "I lost my phone a couple months ago on this bridge, actually. Was walking home at like two in the morning, and I took it out to text this girl I'd met earlier that night, and I dropped it." He pointed at the ground and then laughed. "Hit the concrete and was totally fine because I got this badass case for it when I got it. I totally didn't

expect it to bounce, though." He looked over the railing to the water below. "Anyway, there's some fish down there that has a new iPhone now, and I'm stuck with this refurbished piece of shit because I can't afford anything else." Pulling the phone out of his pocket, he took a few steps closer to Maddox so he could show it to him.

The fact that this kid had pulled over on his way to wherever he'd been headed, combined with him telling Mad about his lost phone, had Maddox unsure of what to do next. He couldn't tell a stranger why he was on the bridge, and he didn't want to be rude by telling him to go away. It occurred to him that he shouldn't care if he sounded rude, because as soon as the kid left, Maddox would cease to exist. To anyone.

The kid was still holding the phone out for Mad to look at, and because Mad couldn't think of anything else to do, he focused his attention on the phone. "Damn. That really is a piece of shit. I thought refurbished ones still came in good condition."

"They do. I fucked this one up too."

The last thing Mad expected himself to do on this bridge was start laughing, but that was exactly what he found himself doing.

The kid joined in before saying, "I was scared to put a case on this one because I didn't want it bouncing away from me again. A cracked phone is better than no phone, I guess. But I don't plan on drinking straight bourbon again anytime soon."

Maddox raised an eyebrow. "Straight bourbon, huh? Seems a little strong for a sixteen-year-old."

"Fuck you," the kid joked. "I'm twenty."

Mad laughed again. "You shouldn't even be drinking yet."

"Well, my parents didn't name me Wilder for nothin'. What are you? One of those dudes who follows all the rules?"

"Guess you could say that. They drilled that mentality into me pretty hard in the army."

"Oh wow. Army? That's awesome." Then Wilder extended a hand and his expression became more serious. "Thank you for your service. I have so much respect for people who join the military or become firefighters or police officers. There's not a hero's bone in my body."

Mad took his hand and shook it hard. "Thanks. Means a lot," he said. "I'm Maddox, by the way."

"Nice to meet you," Wild said before letting go of Mad's hand. "So, Maddox, you gonna tell me what you lost so I can help you find it?"

Mad thought for a few moments, looking into the eyes of a stranger who'd stopped to talk to him when Maddox thought he was completely alone in the world. "Nah. Doesn't matter," he said.

It was the one and only time Maddox had almost quit on something, and that something had been life. Mad picked up the weight two more times before he was able to lock it over his head. When he brought his feet back up to a full standing position, he stood there for a few seconds, wanting to enjoy the feeling of beating his personal best. Then he dropped the bar and began taking the weights off it. Wild went to the other side and did the same.

Maddox had wanted to ask Wild about that night for years, but he hadn't ever brought it up, and neither had Wild. Mad wondered if there was a reason he'd never come clean about why he'd been on the bridge that night, since the men knew everything else about each other. But after what they shared with Jasmine—what they'd both lost—now seemed like as good a time as any. "Can I ask you something?" he said.

Wild looked up from the barbell. "Of course. Anything," he said, clearly sensing Mad's earnestness.

"Did you really lose your phone?"

Wilder looked confused. "What?"

"When you saw me on that bridge," he clarified. "You said you'd dropped your phone over it when you were walking home one night. Did that really happen?"

Wild's expression seemed to sadden at the memory, and he took a few seconds to answer. "Nah. That phone I showed you was the same shitty one I'd had since I graduated high school." A sound that was almost a laugh escaped from him, but he seemed to stifle it.

Mad couldn't help but give him a small smile too.

"You didn't lose anything that night, did you?" Wild asked.

Maddox knew his voice would sound raspy, so he cleared his throat before speaking. He wanted to tell Wild that he'd been wrong when he said he didn't have a hero's bone in his body—that Wilder was more of a hero than he knew—but something told him that he didn't need to speak the words for Wild to know what Mad thought of him. "No," he said. "I almost did, though."

♦♦♦♦

The two men put the rest of the equipment away before locking up the gym and heading over to the bar down the street. Wild wanted to know what had prompted Mad to ask about the night they'd met eight years ago, but Mad had seemingly let the conversation go, and Wild didn't want to bring up old hurts. Not when they had fresh ones to deal with. So instead, Wild turned the conversation to himself. "So I've been thinking about what I said to Jaz."

"What's that?" Mad asked.

"About not being a guy you bring home to your parents and all that."

Mad nodded but said nothing.

"I think it might be something I could ease into."

"I don't know if you can ease into it. You either meet the parents or you don't. There's no middle ground."

"I don't know," Wild said, taking a seat at the bar. "It's only her mom I'd have to meet, so that's only like...half."

Maddox laughed and then ordered them beers when the bartender came over. "When did you get so good at math?"

"Shut up," Wild said, but he laughed too. "I'm serious, though. I think I could try to make this something serious. Ish," he added. "I've been giving it a lot of thought." Though Wilder knew "a lot of thought" for him didn't necessarily equal a normal person's cognitive efforts.

Mad looked interested. "Oh yeah? What made you come to this conclusion?"

Wild spun his beer and traced his finger over the condensation before answering. When he did, he fixed his stare on Maddox, hoping his friend would pick up on the gravity of his words, even though they were simple ones. "I miss her," he said with a shrug. "She's the first woman I've ever felt this way about."

Maddox held Wild's eyes with his own until they both felt the need to look away. "I miss her too."

Both men were quiet for a while before Mad spoke again. "I'm just scared I can't be what she needs. Like I can't give the amount or the part of myself that she deserves." He shook his head, his eyes directed down at the bar, and Wild suspected by the shakiness in Mad's voice that he was holding back tears. "How can someone so fragile be someone's rock?"

"Not sure the 'how' matters. I just know it's possible," Wild said, placing his hand on Mad's shoulder and applying pressure until Mad looked up at him. They'd been best friends for so long, they could both say so much with a look. But Wild knew the words were important too. Maybe the most important, because they spoke of a truth Mad should've already known but clearly didn't. "And I know it's possible because a rock is what you've always been for me."

CHAPTER TWENTY-TWO

Jaz stared out of the second-floor window of Jethro's house, watching the hustle and bustle below as the event crew and caterers hustled around to finish setting up before guests arrived. Jaz had to admit, her mom had outdone herself this time, managing to land a rancher who seemed content to spend his obviously vast wealth on whatever would make her mother happy. And the odd thing was, it seemed as if her mom actually *was* happy. Her mom had always put on a good show during her other weddings, but watching her look at Jethro like he hung the moon simply by existing let Jaz see what true happiness looked like on her mother. It was a decidedly good look on her.

"Jasmine, can you help us zip this? I swear it's going to take the jaws of life to get her into this dress," Isabella grumbled as she gathered as much lace material as she could in her fists and pulled tightly while Ariel inched the zipper up.

"Jesus, Mom, did you lather yourself in Crisco when you tried this thing on?" Ariel asked through gritted teeth as she struggled with the zipper.

Her mom released a put-upon sigh. "The seamstress didn't have nearly this much trouble. You two must be doing something wrong."

"You can't zip a dress wrong," Ariel snapped as she gave up and backed away.

"Goddamnit, Ariel, we almost had it," Isabella growled.

"In your dreams," Ariel muttered.

Despite the fact that the three of them were ready to murder one another, Jaz couldn't help but smile. These women drove her completely insane, but God did she love them. It wasn't until she'd seen them all bickering in Jethro's kitchen the night she'd arrived home that she'd realized how much she'd missed them. Though within twenty-four hours, she'd also realized that missing them was preferable to living anywhere near them ever again.

Jaz stood up, smoothing her pink satin bridesmaid's dress, which was shockingly not shaped like a princess ball gown but rather A-line and simple. "Mom," she said softly. "Raise your arms up and close your eyes."

Her mother hesitated but ultimately did what Jaz asked. Keeping her voice low, Jaz took her mom through some breathing exercises, telling her to imagine herself shedding her stress like a second skin, letting all of the worry exit her body with her next breath and centering herself in the moment. As Jaz spoke, she slowly made her way around her mother and gently took hold of the zipper. "I'm going to count, and when I reach three, I want you to inhale deeply. One. Two." As Jaz said, "Three," her mother took a deep breath, and Jaz eased the zipper halfway up. "Okay, one more time." With the next inhale, Jaz was able to work the zipper all the way to the top and fasten the clasp.

Grasping her mom's shoulder, Jaz turned her so she was

facing the mirror. Jaz rested her chin on her mom's shoulder and let her hands wrap around her biceps. "Open your eyes."

Her mom did and let out a soft gasp as she took in her reflection. She smiled warmly. "Thank you, Jasmine."

"You're welcome, Mom."

Jaz moved to pull away, but her mom reached up and rested a hand on Jaz's. "When this is all done, you and I are going to have a long talk about what's wrong."

Staring at one another in the mirror, Jaz was reminded that despite her mother's crazy preoccupation with fairy tales, she wasn't so caught up in it that she ignored reality. And Anna Mathers-soon-to-be-Busch could read her daughters as if she were a Grimm brother. So Jaz didn't try to play off that she was fine. She simply nodded at her mom before moving away.

"My money is on boy trouble," Ariel said.

Isabella cupped her own chin as she stared at Jaz. "I dunno. Jasmine doesn't usually get like this with boys. Maybe she's having a midlife crisis."

Rolling her eyes, Jasmine scoffed. "I'm twenty-five."

Ariel leaned toward Isabella and stage-whispered, "See how she contradicted your explanation but not mine."

"You're both morons," Jaz sniped before beginning to pick up things around the room in order to appear nonchalant. If their worried looks were anything to go by, Jaz was failing miserably, but they didn't say anything else, so she considered that a win. Truth was, even the thought of Wild and Mad was enough to make her eyes sting. Talking about them with her mom and sisters would make her lose it, and Jaz refused to make today about her.

She was glad she hadn't told her sisters about the guys. She'd wanted to make sure it was going somewhere before she told them she was in a polyamorous relationship. And just when Jaz had thought they'd gotten to that point, just when she'd convinced her mom to let her bring both Mad and Wild, it all went to hell. Luckily, it seemed her mom had kept her word and hadn't told Isabella and Ariel about Jaz's unconventional relationship. Jaz had told her mom that she wanted to be the one to explain it to them, but now there was clearly no need to.

"Oh good, Brice is here," Isabella gushed as she looked out the window. "Mm, he looks damn good in that suit." Brice was the guy Isabella had been dating for the past few months and was completely besotted with.

Ariel rushed over and looked down at the guests accumulating on the lawn. "Perry is with him," she said, pointing out her own boyfriend.

A dull ache formed in Jaz's chest as her sisters talked about how good their boyfriends looked. Wild and Mad would put both of them to shame. It was a petty thought, but it still made Jaz sad that she wouldn't get to show off her two gorgeous men. Busying herself by refolding all of their clothes, Jaz tried to keep her breathing even and her sadness at bay.

"Whoa, who are they?" Ariel asked.

"I don't know," Isabella replied. "Mom, does Jethro have two hot relatives you never told us about?"

"Not that I know of," her mom said as she joined them at the window. "No, I have no idea who they are."

Jaz's heart stuttered in her chest. Hope rumbled up within her, even though she tried to quash it. No way would it be them.

Would it? Jaz tried to steady herself as she made her way to the window and looked down. A gasp flew out of her mouth as she let her gaze take in the two men on the lawn.

Her sisters and mom turned to her, but Jaz ran out of the room before any of them could get a word out. She flew down the stairs and practically ran to the backyard. Her heels clacked against the stone walkway, and she forced herself to slow down before she reached them.

Wild saw her first, elbowing Mad and motioning in her direction. They both turned toward her, Mad in a navy suit and Wild in a charcoal-gray one. Both were cut to perfection, hugging the bulky and muscular frame of Mad and highlighting the slimmer yet still powerful build of Wild. They were the most handsome things she'd ever seen.

She came to a stop in front of them, unsure what to say.

"Wow. You look beautiful," Wild said.

"Absolutely stunning," Mad added.

"Thanks." Jaz was pretty sure she blushed as she tucked a strand of her dark hair behind her ear. "You two look amazing. You should wear suits more often."

Both men smiled at her words, but no one said anything else. Unable to take the silence, Jaz said, "What are you doing here?" The words came out hushed, and part of Jaz wished she could be stronger—angrier. But seeing them, knowing they'd come after all, made her feel all warm inside, even though she tried to hide it.

Mad and Wild exchanged a glance before looking back at her. Mad cleared his throat before he said, "We wanted to be here for you."

Swallowing thickly, Jaz fought to keep her voice steady. "You didn't have to do that. I mean, I appreciate it, but I have family here." Jaz shrugged, unsure what the hell she was even trying to say. It made her feel good to know they cared enough to not want her to be alone, but that wasn't the context she wanted them here in, and it left her feeling worse than it did when they weren't here at all. "The ceremony will be starting soon. I need to go back, but I'll see you after the ceremony, okay?" She started to turn away, needing to get the hell out of there before she lost it.

"Jaz." Wild's voice stopped her, causing her to look back at them. "We didn't want to just be here *for* you," he added. "We wanted to be here *with* you. As your dates. If that's still something you want."

At his words, sensation filled Jaz from every angle. A tear slipped from her eye, and she felt it slide down her cheek. A voice in her head told her not to make it easy on them. To tell them she needed time to reflect on whether or not it was really what she still wanted. They'd hurt her, both of them. They'd stood across from her and made her question everything they'd shared. Made her question her judgment and maturity.

But...for what? Everything she wanted was standing in front of her looking as vulnerable as she'd ever seen them. Maybe it was impetuous or naïve, but what-fucking-ever. Maybe Jaz's mom had more of an impact on her than she'd ever given the woman credit for. Because she was pretty sure her princes were standing in front of her, and Jaz would be damned if she was going to stand in the way of her own fairy tale. "You're sure?" she asked, because she needed them to be certain.

Both of them smiled, and the way they looked at her—like she was everything they'd ever wanted—was almost enough to make her melt on the spot. "Yeah," Mad said. "We're absolutely sure."

Unable to hold back a single second more, she threw herself between them, throwing an arm around each of them. They each wrapped an arm around her, and it was probably the most bizarre hug anyone had ever seen, with Jaz clinging to two giants as both of them buried their faces in either side of her neck and held her tightly. But none of them seemed to be the least bit bothered by the fact that they were embracing in a large crowd of people. She let herself be swept away by all the feelings she had for these two complicated, stubborn men.

Jaz had never been part of anything more perfect.

CHAPTER TWENTY-THREE

Waiting for the wedding to end was fucking torture. Mad put on a smile and did his best to be personable, but he was starting to fail at both. Once the ceremony was over, Jaz introduced Wild and him to her mom. She fumbled a little when it came to saying who they were to her, but Wild was quick to supply the words.

"We're her boyfriends," he said as he extended his hand toward Anna.

To her credit, Jaz's mom seemed to have taken her advance notice to heart and rolled with the news as well as could be expected, shaking both of their hands and telling Jaz they clearly had some more talking to do, before the photographer saved them all from more awkwardness. Anna and her new husband left to pose with the cake, but they were almost instantly replaced by Jaz's sisters, who demonstrated less restraint.

"Both of them?" the older one, Isabella, asked. "Wow, you sure have become an overachiever, Jasmine."

"How does that even work?" Ariel asked.

"And on that note..." Jaz said as she ushered Mad and Wild away from the girls.

It had been a nice wedding, and under different

circumstances, Mad would've probably enjoyed himself. But the fear of almost losing Jaz was still a persistent buzz under his skin, and only getting her alone would put it to rest.

Mad and Wild were standing in a corner of the large tent that had been set up for the reception when Jaz found them after returning from being called away to help her mother. "So...where are you guys staying?" she asked.

"A hotel near the airport."

"Hmm," she said. "I think it's time you showed it to me."

Wild and Mad looked at one another for a second before bursting into action, setting their drinks down on a nearby table and rushing to retrieve their jackets. Mad could hear Jaz laughing from behind them, but he didn't care in the least. In that moment, all he cared about was how quickly they could make it to the hotel.

"Anything you need to grab?" Wild asked.

"Nope. I have my bag ready to go by the front door already."

"You're an angel," he said.

They said goodbyes to Jaz's family before ushering Jaz toward the rental they'd gotten at the airport. "I'll drive," Mad said, opening the driver's door before anyone could argue. "Wild, get in the back with her."

Wild looked at him quizzically for a second before a knowing smirk spread out over his face. Jaz smiled too, and Mad was glad they both seemed to know where his mind was.

He climbed in and turned the car on as Wild and Jaz got settled in the back. Once Mad got them on the road, he glanced in the rearview and said, "We missed you."

"So fucking much," Wild added.

"I missed you guys too."

Mad was glad to hear it, but words weren't enough. He had to show her too. "I'm going to get us back to the hotel, and together we're going to show you how much you mean to us."

Mad saw Wild's eyes shoot to his in the rearview. They hadn't talked about how they were going to handle spending time with Jaz once they reunited, but Mad was suddenly sure of how it needed to be. There would be time for them to each have alone time and reassert their individual relationships later. Right now, they all needed the reminder that they were all in this together.

"But I'm an impatient motherfucker and don't want to wait," Mad continued. "So Wild's going to turn on the light back there and get started on telling you what we should've told you a long time ago."

"And what's that?" Jaz's voice was low and raspy. His girl was good and turned on.

Mad glanced up again and saw Wild cup Jaz's face. "That you're...everything." And with those words, his lips descended on hers. Mad would've been jealous that Wild got to touch her if watching wasn't turning his crank as hard as it was.

Jaz groaned into the kiss and slid one of her hands up his chest until she reached his neck, and then moved her hand behind him and tangled her fingers in his hair.

Mad forced his eyes back on the road, but he couldn't help but sneak glances into the back seat as often as he could. He caught a glimpse of Wild's hands roughly kneading Jaz's breasts over her dress. Watched Wild trail kisses along her jaw and down her neck. "Let me see what she has on under her dress," Mad said, his voice hoarse.

Wild smirked at the rearview mirror before pulling the delicate fabric of Jaz's dress up so it pooled around her waist. She had on what amounted to little more than a scrap of pale pink material. Wild ran his fingertips along the fabric and looked to Mad.

"Make her feel as good as she makes us feel," Mad ordered.

Wild didn't waste any time, sliding the thong to the side and rubbing his index finger over her clit.

Jaz immediately tensed at the sensation, reaching her hand out and gripping Wild's forearm, not to stop him but seemingly more to brace herself.

Wild brought his fingers to his mouth and licked them before returning them to toy with her clit again. Jaz was writhing under his ministrations.

"Get her close, but don't let her come." Mad wanted her to fall apart with both of their hands on her. And both of their cocks in her if she was game for that.

Mad concentrated on the road, set on getting them to the hotel as fast as fucking possible. He knew Wild was finger-fucking Jaz, because the keening sound she'd made when he'd entered her had made Mad look in the mirror, but otherwise he'd kept his eyes on the road.

It didn't take them long to arrive at their hotel, and Mad was fucking grateful. He sped into the parking lot and pulled into a spot so quickly his tires squealed. He turned in his seat and looked at Jaz, who was panting as Wild lavished attention on her pussy. "We're here," Mad said since they seemingly hadn't noticed.

Jaz's eyes opened and connected with Mad's.

"Can you walk?" he asked her.

She nodded slowly, almost as if she was drunk.

"I think you should be asking me that question," Wild muttered as he adjusted himself.

"Suck it up, buttercup. We have hours of groveling ahead of us."

Jaz's eyes widened. "Hours?"

Mad smirked. "Hours. Maybe even days." And if they were lucky, maybe they'd even have a lifetime.

CHAPTER TWENTY-FOUR

The three of them stood stock-still in the elevator, as if the slightest movement would break their restraint and make them pounce. And the last thing this night needed was getting arrested for fucking in an elevator. Wild watched the numbers change above the doors as they passed each floor. *Jesus, did Mad get a room on the top fucking floor?*

Finally, they arrived and exited with the decorum of bank robbers trying to play it cool. When they got to their room, Mad slipped the keycard into the lock, opened the door, and headed inside. Wild was the last one to enter, and he pushed the door shut with a force that was unnecessary but seemed pivotal in this moment. The banging of the door broke the levees between them, and Mad pushed Jaz back into Wild as Mad attacked her mouth.

Wild ran his hands all over her and nipped at her neck as she kissed Maddox with fervor. It reminded Wild of the night in the club all those weeks ago. But tonight was about so much more than a shared drunken kiss. Tonight was a claiming.

Wild slowly started moving, guiding Mad and Jaz toward the bed. Feeling Jaz step out of her shoes, Wild decided to get on board the get-Jaz-naked train. He slipped his hands under the strings of her dress and dragged them off her shoulders, causing her gown to fall to the floor. He unhooked her strapless bra next, which also fluttered to the floor as they walked. Wild was just about to reach down to remove her thong, but Mad got there first, taking the bit of fabric in his hands and ripping it from her body. “Show-off,” Wild grumbled.

Mad only hummed in reply, but he turned Jaz so that she was facing Wild. Wild took over kissing her. He registered Mad stripping in his peripheral vision, so Wild took his hands off Jaz so he could begin to do the same.

She got in on the action, unbuttoning his shirt before it evidently got too tedious and she tore it open, causing buttons to clatter to the floor.

“Hmm, somebody’s been lifting,” Wild joked.

“I have. You guys are a terrible influence,” she teased before reconnecting their mouths.

Wild felt Jaz press farther into him and opened his eyes to see that Mad was at her back. Jaz reached a hand back and wrapped it around the nape of Mad’s neck, pulling him closer so he could suck on her neck. Mad moved as if he was rubbing his cock along the crease of Jaz’s ass, and the way Jaz was moaning let Wild know that was exactly what he was doing. Wild undid his belt and pushed his pants and briefs off, kicking off his shoes and stepping out of the last of his clothes.

They were all writhing together, both men rubbing their bodies against Jaz. But suddenly, Mad stopped and took hold of Jaz’s chin and turned her head slightly. “Are you okay with this?”

Wild knew what he was asking. They’d all been present during intimate moments before, but this was the first time they'd all be actively participating. Wild held his breath as he waited for Jaz to answer. When she nodded, Wild exhaled heavily.

"I need your words, Jaz," Mad said, and Wild was thankful at least one of them was responsible, even if he wanted to punch Mad in the face for stopping them.

"Yes. I want this. Both of you," she replied.

"How do you want us?" Mad asked.

"I want one of you to fuck my pussy while the other fucks my mouth."

Wild saw a shiver work through Mad at her words, but he simply nodded to her. He then looked at Wild expectantly. "Me too," Wild said. "It has to be the three of us." It wouldn't always be. It wouldn't even typically be. As much as Wild got off on watching Mad and Jaz together—and knew that Mad felt the same—the relationships would always ultimately be separate. But tonight, and maybe special occasions in the future, the three of them together was necessary. They needed to reforge the bond they'd almost broken. And it would take all three of them to make it strong again.

Satisfied, Mad stepped back and reached down to grab his wallet. He extracted a condom and handed it to Wild before climbing on the bed so that he was kneeling by the headboard. Wild and Jaz didn't need any further instructions. Jaz got on all fours and took Mad's hard cock into her mouth, moaning around it like it was the best thing she'd ever tasted. Wild suited up and then got behind her, running his hands over her ass for a second before lining up and pushing into her in one long thrust.

Jaz groaned but never stopped sucking Mad's cock. Wild didn't move for a second, letting Jaz find a rhythm with both of them inside her. She raised one hand so she could jerk Mad while she said, "Are you going to fuck me or what?" Then she descended on him again without missing a beat.

Wild didn't need to be told twice. He pulled back and thrust back in, causing Jaz's mouth to take more of Mad's cock. The ultimate example of control, Mad didn't move—probably worried about giving Jaz more than she could handle—instead letting Jaz bob up and down on him.

A few times, as Wild began fucking her in earnest, she'd replace her mouth with her hand and lick his length. The sight made Wild excited to be on that end of things. Later. For now, he had a tight pussy contracting around him, reminding him he was exactly where he wanted to be.

She was so turned on that she was nearly dripping with her arousal, making Wild's cock glide in and out of her tight channel easily. Watching where his cock disappeared into her body entranced him. That sight combined with how she felt around him and the sounds she was making turned him into a madman. His thrusts gained intensity, his hips snapping against her pussy with every push.

"That's it," he heard Mad say. The words drew Wild's eyes up the bed to where Mad held Jaz's hair out of the way so she could suck him without impediment.

Jaz popped off his cock and moaned long and low. The sound went right to Wild's balls, making his need to orgasm all the more pressing. "Oh, oh, oh," Jaz chanted as she jacked Mad and pushed back on Wild. "Feels so good. Love being between you."

Her words sent a zing down Wild's spine. "You close?" he asked her.

"So close. So, so close."

Mad reached under her and began toying with her nipples. "Get her there, Wild."

Challenge fucking accepted. Wild began to buck into her with faster, shorter thrusts. He became unaware of anything that wasn't his dick fucking into Jaz. His grip on her hips was tight, and he felt her tense and then shudder before she yelled her release.

The walls of her pussy convulsed around him, squeezing him tightly, the friction amazing on his cock. He gave her two more sharp thrusts before he pushed deep and came, emptying into the condom. His body shook with the intensity of his orgasm, even as he gave a couple more shallow thrusts to empty his cock completely.

His climax had whited-out his brain for who the hell knew how long, but he slowly came back to himself. He was still seated inside Jaz, and Mad was still by her head, though he'd clearly found his release as well. Wild gingerly withdrew from Jaz, tied off the condom, and threw it into a nearby trash can before collapsing onto the bed next to Jaz. Mad scooted around so that he could lie down on her other side.

They rested in comfortable silence for a bit before Jaz flipped over onto her back and spoke. "That...was amazing."

Wild pressed a kiss to her shoulder. "It sure was."

"The first of many amazing adventures together," Mad added.

Jaz laughed. "You guys just double-teamed me after my

mom's wedding. I'm not sure the term adventure even captures it."

Wild joined her in her laughter. "What would you call it, then?"

She turned thoughtful for a second. "A *mis*adventure." She turned so she could smile at each of them in turn. "Well, it's definitely not your average adventure, is it?"

Wild heard Mad let out a chuckle—it was a contented sound. "I can live with that."

"Me too," Wild added. "Me too."

ALSO AVAILABLE FROM
WATERHOUSE PRESS

Keep reading for an excerpt!

EXCERPT FROM
MISADVENTURES WITH MY EX

WEST

Los Angeles

October

"If that son of a bitch hadn't given in to his case of cold feet, I would be on a beach somewhere—like Bora Bora or Bali or Barbados. Why do all the best beaches start with a B?"

As I look through the small, airy apartment, I can't see the woman who slurs the words, but I'd know Eryn Hope's voice anywhere.

"I would be soaking up the sun, enjoying my life, and glowing from multiple orgasms because, even though Weston Quaid is a total bastard, he was always amazing in bed."

My former fiancée's younger sister, Echo, stands in the open door, wincing. "You didn't hear that."

Though I'd rather not be here, and I probably should have come equipped with a steel-girded jockstrap and a shield to protect myself from what I suspect will be a shit fight, I can't not grin. "Not a word."

"But *nooo*. I'm getting romantic with Ernest and Julio Gallo. They don't give orgasms." Eryn huffs. "Hey, if that was the pizza guy who rang the doorbell, bring me a slice, will you? I need something to soak up this merlot."

"Eryn is just...having a bad day," Echo murmurs.

Because life in general has been rough or because, if things had ended differently, my former fiancée and I would be celebrating our third wedding anniversary tonight?

"I understand."

Truthfully, today has sucked for me, too. I've avoided thinking about the significance of this date since I woke up. Too many what-ifs and memories. Since I walked away from Eryn, I've fought a gritty, ugly uphill battle. It's almost over. I seem to be winning now...but along the way, I've taken terrible losses.

"Maybe you should go." Echo begins to close the door. "She's not exactly sober."

I wedge my foot past the threshold. "Waiting isn't an option. I need to see your sister tonight. It's business."

Echo frowns. "What business could you two possibly have? Eryn won't want to see you now. Maybe not ever."

I'm not surprised. Or deterred. "I—"

"Pizza?" A teenage kid wearing a collared shirt with a well-known chain's logo dashes up the stairs, an insulated carrier balanced on his palm.

I take out my wallet and pay the guy, tipping handsomely so this interruption will go away.

"Thanks!" the high schooler calls over his shoulder as he runs back down the steps.

"You didn't have to do that," Echo insists, cash in hand.

"I'd like to deliver this to your sister personally. Alone."

Echo hesitates. She's usually free-spirited, funny, and easy-breezy. Once, we shared a good camaraderie. Not surprisingly, that's gone. Hell, I'm shocked she's speaking to me at all.

As usual, she's dressed as if she belongs in a granola commercial. Today, it's braids and flannel, cargo shorts, knee socks, and hiking boots. She's an original. But she's also fiercely protective of both her older sisters, just as they're protective of her.

"I don't know if she can handle that," Eryn's sister admits. "To be honest, this day is rough on her every year."

I've come to dread October fourth, too. My younger brother, Flynn, pointed out this morning that the first year after my split with Eryn wrecked me, but he's relieved I got over her.

Clearly, I have him fooled.

But I'm not here to win Eryn back. And after the way our split went down, I'm sure that's impossible.

"Your sister bought a restaurant recently. I need to talk to her about it. Only talk," I assure Echo. "I'll make sure she gets fed, sobered up, and safely in bed. No fighting. Just conversation. I'll keep my hands to myself." *Even if I'm dying to touch her.*

"Echo, where's the damn pizza?" Eryn calls again from somewhere deeper in her apartment. "If I have to eat mediocre pie instead of fresh seafood on the freaking beach in the Bahamas—see, another great beach that starts with a B—I'd like it hot."

"Coming." But Echo doesn't move, simply blinks at me.

Is she surprised I know about Eryn's new endeavor? Gauging my sincerity? Probably both.

"Echo, I wouldn't ask to see her, especially tonight, if it wasn't important."

Finally, she sighs and lets me inside. "All right. Only because I don't think she'll ever move on until you two have talked."

Guilt stings. I handled our breakup horribly. True, I'd been blindsided and was reeling myself. I've been over those dark days in my head a thousand times. I can't change how everything unfolded now, and I didn't come here to rehash the past, but maybe while I handle business I can give her some peace.

"Thank you."

Echo lingers. "So, you're a bigwig CEO now?"

I can't miss her subtle dig. "Yes."

"Congratulations...I guess."

She's judging me for seemingly prioritizing business above love. I get it. That's not exactly true, but I understand it must appear that way. At the time, I made the only choice I thought I could. Only distance and perspective have made me second-guess that.

"How's school?" I change the subject. "You're close to finishing, right?"

"I graduate in May, then after my internship I'll be

adulting full-time." Her grim smile melts into a frown. "Be good to my sister. Don't make me regret showing you mercy. Tell her I'll call her tomorrow."

"Of course."

Without another word, she grabs her overstuffed wallet, knit ski cap, and giant chain of dangling key rings, then nods as she closes the door behind her with a quiet snick.

After three long years, I'm alone with Eryn Hope. Maybe I'll have the chance to apologize for what I can't control now...and what I didn't know how to stop then. She might understand. But I'm realistic. This is Eryn. Thanks to a chaotic childhood with workaholic parents, she was cynical even before we met. I can only imagine how guarded she'll be now.

After all, I left her on our wedding day.

I step past the stylishly lived-in kitchen and deeper into the apartment that has a vintage, Audrey Hepburnesque vibe. It's so Eryn. My heart thumps madly the closer I come to her. Not surprising. After all, losing her was the worst mistake I ever made. Not a day goes by that I don't think of her.

"What's taking so long?" she calls. From the bedroom, maybe?

She's moved since our engagement. We both have. The apartment we shared here in LA was probably too full of ghosts and memories for her to remain. And after more than two years in New York, I've now settled in Las Vegas.

"Echo, you're listening, right? I'm pouring my heart out," Eryn continues with a sigh. "You know what sucks more? It's like that bastard ruined me. I can't orgasm with anyone else. And—oh, god—I still masturbate to thoughts of him. What's wrong with me?"

It might make me an asshole, but I don't hate knowing that no one else has pleased Eryn's sweet, petite curves as well as I did. In fact, I swell with more than masculine pride when I remember all the ways I once wrung screams from her.

I wish I could have even one night with my ex again.

On soft footfalls, I cross the kitschy-chic black-and-white living room, then find the bedroom tucked away through an alcove on the right. I lean against the doorframe, shoulder braced, and watch as my deepest regret paces the small bedroom in bare feet—and adorned in the wedding dress I never had the pleasure of seeing her wear.

I wish like hell we'd made it to the altar so I'd have the right to put my arms around her, kiss her neck, and seduce her straight into bed. Logically, I know the smartest course of action now would be to give her the unfortunate news about the property that houses her restaurant, then maybe broach an honest conversation about our past before I leave her in peace. Maybe afterward we'd both be able to heal and be happy.

Because the woman in front of me clearly isn't. And for that, I'm beyond sorry.

"There's nothing wrong with you, honey," I tell her. "I still think of you, too. All the time."

Eryn whirls with a gasp, a nearly empty bottle of red wine in hand. "West?"

When our stares meet, it's a sucker punch to my solar plexus. I stare at her haunting dark eyes in her shocked pale face. She blinks. Her rosy lips part as if she means to speak, but she doesn't say another word.

My former fiancée is even more beautiful than before. How is that possible?

"Hi," I say, my voice rough.

"This can't be happening. I haven't seen you in three years, and now I'm suddenly seeing two of you?" She shakes her head. "No. You're a hallucination. You'll go away."

Repressing a smile, I set the warm pizza box on her rumpled bed, trying not to notice that the sheets smell like Eryn. Baby powder and vanilla and something musky that always turned me on. I've never experienced a similar fragrance on any other woman. I can't identify it, but I know it well. That scent takes me back. It makes me instantly hard.

"I'm not a product of the wine or your imagination, Eryn."

"You have to be. You look like West. You sound like him. You're hot like him." She shakes her head. "But my sister knows better than to let you into my place. Echo!"

"She's gone. She'll call you in the morning. It's just us here...and what I assume is a sausage, mushroom, and onion pizza." At least based on the savory aroma. "I came to talk to you."

Her eyes narrow. "I don't care that fake-you remembers what I like to eat. Go. You're not welcome here."

"We have to talk." I approach with slow steps.

Eryn backs up, shaking her head. "Stop."

I do.

She snorts. "Now I know you're not real. Turns out, the West I was engaged to didn't give a shit about me or what I wanted."

No doubt she saw it that way. "Can we sit down and eat? Be civil? I'd like to apologize and explain why I'm here. Will you listen?"

ERYN

I blink. Then blink again.

Nope, Weston Quaid is still standing in my bedroom, looking really, really real—and really, really gorgeous. He still thinks of me? Ha! I don't believe that for a minute. How can I? Besides, if he wants to apologize, he must be a mirage.

Except...when did my visions of West ever include him sporting a perfectly tailored suit, a well-kept beard, and dark hair cut ruthlessly short?

"I'm not spending tonight with you, especially not an imaginary version. That would make me pitiful. And I'm not. I'm just drunk." I tip the bottle to my lips and imbibe another swallow of the mellow red. "Once I'm sober, you'll be gone."

That kind of depresses me.

How many times have I fantasized that West would show up and say he's sorry? Too many. Still, I'm not listening tonight. If I let myself believe he's actually here to make amends for walking out on our wedding day, I'll cry again. I've already done too much of that.

"Eryn." Softly, he cups my shoulder. "I'm staying until we've talked."

At his touch, I'm uncomfortably aware of a dark, unwelcome heat suffusing my every muscle and nerve. It centers into a throbbing ache in one unmistakable place. The sensations make me feel even more woozy...but I'll never be drunk enough to forget that he was the cause of the most humiliating, heartbreaking time in my life.

The contact also proves he's really, truly standing in the middle of my bedroom, his gaze fixed on me.

"Why?" On this day, of all days? "If you came to find out whether gullible little Eryn is still a train wreck over the split, you can see I'm fine."

He raises an expressive dark brow at me. "So...it's normal for you to be drunk, wearing your wedding dress, and lamenting about your sad sex life since I've gone?"

"You *heard* that?" As mortification rolls over me, I raise the bottle of wine to my lips for more liquid fortification.

West plucks it from my hand and shoves it onto the dresser behind him, out of my reach. "Eryn, we have a lot to say. Give me an hour. I know you don't owe me anything, but if you'll let me say my piece, I'll leave for good."

"Of course you will. You're an expert at that." I wave a dramatic hand through the air. "I remember all the times I 'gave you an hour' and you made my toes curl. Which was awesome; I'm not gonna lie. But then, after everything? Poof. You were gone with nothing more than an 'I'm sorry, honey.'"

"Eryn—"

"Do you know how many people I had to explain our breakup to? I lost count. At first, I told people about your family emergency, but after a while... What was I supposed to say? You didn't explain why you never came back. So I told people how great it was that we realized we weren't compatible before we exchanged vows. It would have served you right if I'd told everyone you had a raging case of herpes." I huff, still trying to comprehend that the one man I thought I'd love, honor, and cherish forever is standing in front of me. "I mailed back gifts and sent a retraction to the paper about our wedding announcement. I canceled everything—and I didn't want your stupid check. I tore it up and paid for everything myself. And while we're at it, this is yours, too." I march to my nightstand and pull out the burgundy velvet box West gave me one hot July evening. All was perfect with the world then... I toss it at him now, gratified it hits him square in the chest. "Take it and go."

West catches the little box, then opens it to find the engagement ring nestled inside, still sparkling and winking in the light. It always mocks me with what might have been, so I stopped looking at it long ago. Mostly.

He sets it on the bed. "This is yours, Eryn. Keep it. I never expected you to give it back."

"But you never expected to slide the matching wedding band on my finger, either, did you? Now that I know you're filthy rich, I guess you're not too broken up about spending thirty thousand on a ring." When he opens his mouth, I wave his words away. "Whatever you're going to say, I don't care. You and I are ancient history, and nothing will change the fact you turned out to be an asshat whose best talent lies between the sheets." I grit my teeth. "Ugh, I have to stop pumping up your ego. If I could get a decent sex life, that would help, but I'm still better off without you. So just go. I'm going to eat my pizza and watch a marathon of *La Femme Nikita*. Or *Kill Bill*. Blood and guts will make me feel better."

"You hate violent movies."

He remembered that, too. That makes me even sadder. Once upon a time, I swore we were perfect for each other. "Maybe since I learned to hate you, I've learned to love them."

As soon as I spit the words out, I clap my mouth shut. Damn it, I don't want to be combative, emotional, or bitter. Booze and West combined have killed my composure.

No, I threw it out the window. Somewhere in my head, I realize I'm not acting like a grown-up. I'd love to be mad at him for that, too. But it's my fault...with some help from merlot.

"I'm sorry." He pins me with solemn eyes. "That I left you with a mess. That I didn't explain. Most of all, I'm sorry that I hurt you."

His sincerity penetrates my alcohol armor. Tears prick my eyes. God, I don't want to be vulnerable to Weston Quaid ever again. "Fine. Apology accepted. Now will you go away?"

He shakes his head. "I can't."

This story continues in
Misadventures with My Ex!

MORE MISADVENTURES

VISIT MISADVENTURES.COM
FOR MORE INFORMATION!